Ann LeBlanc
THE TRANSITIVE PROPERTIES OF CHEESE
Neon Hemlock Press

NEON HEMLOCK

Neon Hemlock Press
www.neonhemlock.com
@neonhemlock

The Transitive Properties of Cheese
Ann LeBlanc

Cover Illustration by Drew Shields
Interior Illustrations by Matthew Spencer
Cover Design and Layout by dave ring
Interior Design and Layout by dave ring
Edited by dave ring

Print ISBN-13: 978-1-952086-86-1
Ebook ISBN-13: 978-1-952086-87-8

THE TRANSITIVE PROPERTIES OF CHEESE

BY ANN LEBLANC

*To Cora — my love for you is baked in to every word I write.
To Arthur — I love your stories, your imagination,
and most importantly, you.*

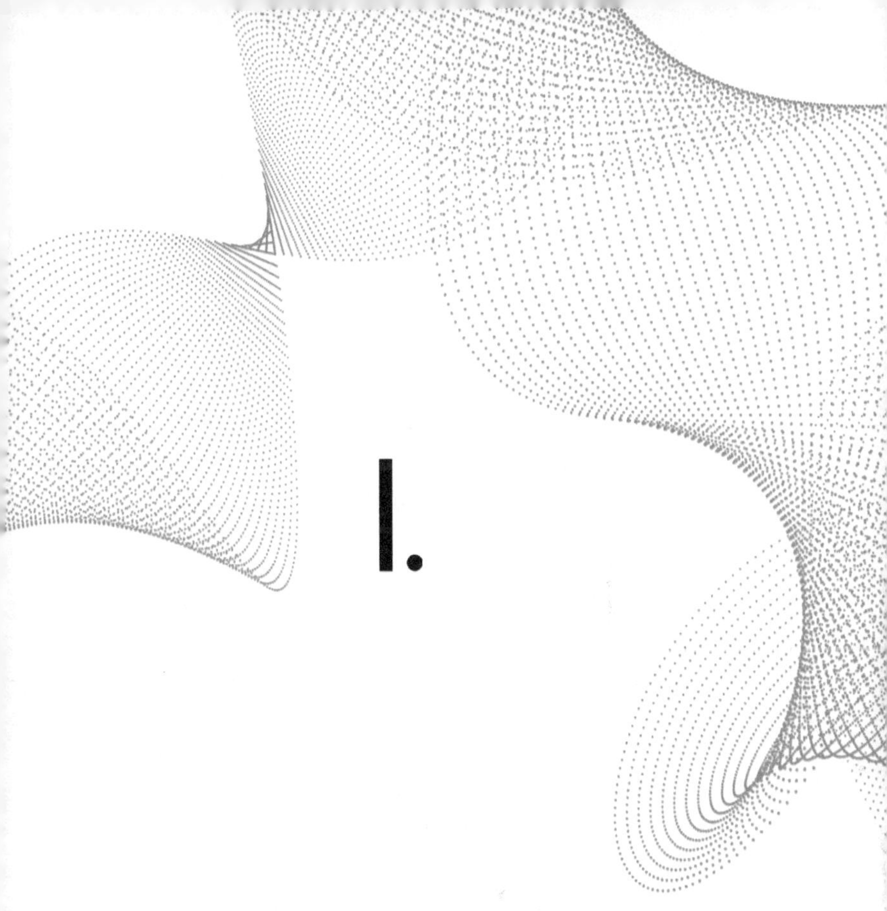

I.

MILLIONS WAYLAND WAS cutting the curds when she learned someone had thrown her cheese cave into the sun.

She was only half listening to the newsfeed; most of her attention was submerged down into the piezo-electric nerves and lean plastiform muscles of her work-body. It was important to feel the process with her whole self, to hear the cheese speaking to her through the millions of sensors built into the body she'd designed. Her four heat-resistant rubberized hands felt the slip and bounce of the curds in their bath, holding them as gently as a mother holds a child; her smart nose reveled in the smell of curdle and cream. It was so easy in this body to let the work encompass her wholly.

So when the newsfeed dispassionately mentioned that asteroid L3-5961 had been diverted into a terminally decaying orbit, she didn't immediately recognize the alphanumeric designation. It took a long moment before understanding dropped like rennet through the waters of her mind, curdling her thoughts into confusion, fear, rage.

The cave was integral to her process; it was where her cheeses ripened from something soft and fresh with a simple flavor profile into something far more rich and complex. A part of her screamed to tip over the curdling basin, to trash the workshop, but there were fifteen batches to finish after this one, and if she was about to lose her cheese cave, she couldn't afford to wreck her workshop too. She locked herself out of her body's motor control for thirty seconds, and scream-howled her frustration, raw noise echoing against the utilitarian stainless-steel walls of her orbital workshop.

A thirty-second break was luxury enough. The whey needed to be drained and the curds needed to be packed. After that, she had more batches to complete. But every moment she delayed, her cheese cave hurtled closer to the all-consuming sun. How long did she have before solar radiation began to overwhelm the carefully tuned temperature management systems, cooking the delicate ecosystem of beneficial microorganisms? How long before it became too expensive to hire a tug to reverse the asteroid's deadly decaying orbit? Two weeks? Maybe three?

She was willing to bet all the cheese she'd ever made that Miller was the one who'd done this. He owned the asteroid; caring for the messy logistical details while she made cheese was *his* responsibility.

But Miller wouldn't answer her messages. For every <We need to talk,> and <What did you do with my cheese cave?> she got back an automated <In a meeting, talk later.> Unacceptable. If she let herself get distracted by her work, later could easily transform into too late.

If Miller wouldn't talk to her, she needed to transmit herself over to his office on Lenaius Station and yell at him in-person. But that would mean abandoning her work. She needed another set of hands, another self, and that meant doing what she'd sworn to never do again: copy herself.

Wayland gave herself the luxury of fifteen minutes procrastinating—draining the whey, gently placing the jiggling curds in presses—before she connected to the space-station's emulation systems and initiated the self-copy process. She hesitated when the system asked her to confirm informed-consent. It had been nineteen years since she'd last copied herself. Did she dare, after what had happened all those years ago at Crestfall?

She aborted the copy process, returned to the cheese. Her thoughts looped, circling the drain of her loss. She restarted the copy-process, closed it again. Nine times she did this, until she realized her indecision itself was delaying her work, and in a brief moment of courage she confirmed consent.

The station's emulation systems locked her out of her body's sensor and motor-control systems. For a terrible lonely moment she was a mind floating free in the formless void. This might have been relaxing, except for the anticipated horror of the next stage in the copy process. *Please be quick*, she chanted soundlessly to the void. *Please be—*

The clamp took hold, freezing her thoughts in a frozen jittery loop, gripping her static as the worms came in. Ten-thousand needles thrashed through her thoughts, slowly, agonizingly consuming her and replicating her mind. Raw and tattered, she felt every gnawing worm, every doubled sensation, every copied memory.

When the process was done, she shuddered. Her body floated ephemeral in the station's emulation space, semi-translucent and not really physically there. Her other self stood in her work-body, watching her with its unexpressive utilitarian face. So, she was the copy this time.

The two Waylands flinched, averting their eyes, both feeling the same mix of emotions. Neither wanted to deal with the messy aftermath of copying. No point in choosing names, updating the Millions registry, or deciding roles and rules. The last time they'd done this, the last time she'd been on Lenaius, disaster had followed. Thankfully, the only thing at stake this time was her cheese.

"Wayland," Wayland said, talking to the original who'd already gotten back to work. "I'll be back soon, hopefully. Don't forget to add more rennet to the next resupply order." She assumed this would be a quick split. Her original would finish the cheese-making, and the copy would deal with Miller and the cheese-cave. Ideally, it would take no more than a few hours. Any more, and she might accrue too many Unique Life Experiences, which would prevent reintegration.

The original Wayland didn't answer, she had already fallen into the reverie of the work. The copy shrugged her ghostly shoulders. This was why they'd copied themself. There was always more work, and there were always more copies to do that work.

She took a simulated deep breath, counted to three, and then initiated the transmission of her digitally emulated mind across the empty kilometers of space. Compared with the copy-process, transmission felt like nothing at all. A brief lacuna of consciousness, and then she awoke in an arrival booth on Lenaius Co-Op Station and Trans-Orbital Hub, floating translucent in the station's emulation space. Lenaius was one of the oldest and largest stations orbiting Earth, and one of the last to still be mostly autonomous.

She breathed in the simulated smell of the station—that indescribable mix of off-gassing plastics, human breath and sweat, layered with the burnt-steak smell of a recently used space-dock—and tried not to remember the last time she was here. More than five thousand unread messages winked angrily at the top of her vision, reminding her of how much everyone here probably still hated her.

Her brain—the digital copy of it she'd transmitted to Lenaius—was running on the station's emulation servers. The servers piped sensory information—gathered from hardpoint cameras and swarms of ever-present micro-drones—that told her brain she was in the booth. Anyone with AR goggles or implants could see her body, rendered semi-translucent so no-one tried to touch or lean on her. The tech dated back to the early multi-instantiation experiments, and was extremely useful for travel within the station archipelago that stretched like scattered plastic debris on the ocean surface between Venus, Earth, Mars, and the asteroid belt—where the distances involved made physical travel and transmission latency a serious problem.

Emulation space was good enough for a quick visit, but she needed a body. Otherwise it would be too easy for Miller to ignore her. His restaurant was one of the few places on the station excluded from emulation space due to the anxieties of tourists from Earth. But renting a body would be too expensive and impersonal. She needed to borrow one of her other selves for this.

"I'M ON A date," her other self said when Wayland's ghostly visage appeared at her table. Her other self—who the Million's registry ID'd as Millions Hattie—wore a fat organic body, clad high-femme in an amaranthine ode to cotton candy. Shimmer-tattoos of people lounging, drinking, and laughing danced up and down her arms, but the whole effect of her bubbly presentation was ruined by her peeved, insincere smile (which Wayland admitted was entirely her own fault). Hattie's date wore tweed, a tattoo of the Pleiades on her forehead, and a large wineglass at her lips. Two bowls of soup sat steaming at the table, the restaurant bustle-loud around them.

"I need to borrow your body. It's urgent. Wait—can they see me?" Wayland asked, gesturing at the date. She looked like the sort of person who might be un-augged.

The date raised an eyebrow, eyes trailing up and down Wayland's ethereal four-armed work-body. "I didn't think I'd meet another one of you so soon. I've never dated a… multi-instantiated before." They pronounced the archaic term carefully, like they were afraid of making offense.

Hattie rolled her eyes. "This is…" Her eyes went distant, presumably checking the registry. "Oh! Wayland, the cheesemaker. How unexpected. But she's just leaving, isn't she?" Hattie turned towards Wayland. "Look, I've got *plans* for tonight, so I will literally pay you to fuck off and rent a utili-skeleton."

"It's a pleasure to meet you." Wayland offered an ethereal salute to the date, then turned to Hattie. "I don't want a generic body. Miller fucked me over, and I want to yell at him wearing one of mine. In person, where he can't ignore my messages." Miller was notorious for avoiding uncomfortable confrontations.

Hattie's eyes widened, and she put on an exaggerated show of thinking it over, stroking her chin like an old wizard. "Miller? Really? And you can get me into his office? And I get to watch you yell at him?" She grinned wide. "Sure, I'm in. But first, soup."

Wayland considered. On the one hand, every moment she delayed, her cheese cave hurtled another umpty-dozen kilometers closer to the sun. On the other hand, Wayland had heard of this restaurant, had wanted to try it for years, but hadn't been brave enough or had enough free time to leave her workshop. The chef had partnered with Lenaius Station's recycler guild to grow mushrooms on discarded organic bodies (whether injured, old, or unwanted). The corpse-mushrooms were then fermented and used to make a clear broth that was both bright and funky.

"Deal. Soup first. But you have to let me have a bite. A big bite. Three bites."

Hattie laughed and pinged Wayland with an invitation to transfer from emulation-space to her organic body. It had been a long time since Wayland had ridden in another Millions' body, and so when Hattie let her in, the rush of sensation made her gasp with Hattie's mouth and shiver with her muscles. Wearing an organic body felt so different from her work-body, all sensations simultaneously imprecise and intense, raw and involuntary. Hattie's parietal-lobe implant allowed Wayland's emulated mind to operate separately in parallel from Hattie's own mind, but they shared all the same sensory data, and as much motor control as Hattie was willing to give Wayland.

They slurped up the soup together, sharing every sensation. The food was even better than she expected: pickled peppers, braised cabbage, thick bouncy rice-noodles, all topped with blackened-garlic oil. It was the best meal—actually, the only meal—Wayland had eaten in a long time. Her work-body back at the workshop was fully synthetic: no digestive system, no distractions from the needs of the flesh, just the glorious all-consuming work.

When the soup had been reduced to a puddle at the bottom of the bowl, and the last drop of wine had been drunk, Hattie jumped up and embraced her date, not bothering to kick Wayland out of their shared body. At the first electric touch of lip on lip, Wayland yelped and leapt back into emulation space. It was too much, too soon, and she didn't have time to get caught up in an erotic doubling experience. Hattie laughed—throaty, gleeful—and made her kisses ostentatiously sloppy.

They'd already wasted too much time eating; Wayland tapped her foot impatiently, which didn't have quite the same effect when her foot was emulated.

ON THE WAY to Miller, Wayland accepted Hattie's invitation to re-enter her body. She needed to accustom herself to feeling how she walked with short legs and wide hips; how the faint caressing breeze of the station's ventilation system left goosebumps on her soft skin; the foreign proprioception of unfamiliar muscles moving ligament and bone.

"This is a good body," Wayland said to herself.

"Yea," Hattie said, and Wayland felt their shared mouth curl into a grin. The sensation of those soft lips resting on one another was overwhelming. "I designed it myself, birthed it myself. It's me, and I love it."

"That must've been expensive. You own, or rent?"

Hattie added a little swagger to their step, and Wayland fell in love with the sway of her hips. "Oh, I'm free and clear. Did you not read my registry bio before you interrupted my date?"

"Well, er…" Wayland mumbled, too embarrassed to admit she'd barely glanced at the registry bio. She'd been in too much of a hurry. This was a bit of a faux-pas among Millions. At the very least, she should've made sure Hattie wasn't a copy-descendent of someone dangerous, or someone who might still hold a grudge about Crestfall. Instead, she'd just picked the first Millions on the station list who had their location public.

Wayland pulled up the registry, but before it loaded, Hattie said, "I'm the elected hetwoman for the 'Nysus Cult and Restaurant Group."

"Oh fuck," Wayland whispered with Hattie's lips. The registry confirmed it; her other self wasn't just rich enough to afford to live-birth her own body, she was one of Miller's primary rivals in the orbital hospitality industry. Further back in the bio revealed Hattie was a copy-descended of Riley-of-the-Fountain—who Wayland remembered as a hardcore sensualist. Not Wayland's first choice, but better by far than a true radical like a Waverian or a spiritual descendent of the Nine Martyrs.

"Is Miller gonna recognize you?" Wayland didn't need this day to get any more complicated.

Hattie laughed, the sound like magic to Wayland, who felt it with her whole body. "Have you ever known Miller to have the smallest amount of self-awareness? You know he won't even look at the registry. He's never seen this body—it's my party-body not my business-body. And I would *never* party with that asshole."

HATTIE WAS A firm believer in divine providence. How else could she explain this delicious morsel of a Millions copy dropping out the sky right into her lap? She was going to have so much *fun* with this cheesemaker. Even better, she'd be able to piggyback off Wayland's registry ID to get access to that impossible prick, Miller. Divine providence, surely. An extra-large offering to lady D was in order tonight.

Miller's office was in the crown jewel of his hospitality empire, the House of the Cosmic Palate. Hattie thought the name was incredibly ironic, given its bland and unimaginative take on Neo-Minimalist cuisine. It served the sort of food only rich tourists could enjoy, which was part of the reason the reservation list was booked up years out. She wasn't jealous though; she had *no* desire for *that* sort of clientele.

It was dinnertime according to the station's artificial time-zone, so the front of the house rang with the sound of laughter and clinking cutlery. Guests in drab Earth-style clothes waited to be checked in at the host stand, which a plaque proclaimed to be made from real Earth redwood—what a waste.

Hattie rolled her eyes at Wayland—who steered their body to the back of the queue—and then grabbed motor control back so she could cut the line. An old woman wearing more pearls than sense scoffed at her, then gasped, offended, afraid, when Hattie stuck her tongue out and flashed the whites of her eyes.

"I'm here to see Miller," Wayland said, voice unsteady either because she wasn't used to Hattie's body or because she was flustered from Hattie taking charge. "It's me, Wayland."

The host stared at her blankly, not recognizing the body or the name of the woman who made cheese for Miller. She put her finger to her temple, the universal sign for *I'm sending a message on my implant.* "He's in a meeting. Do you want me to write down your message?" The host held a pencil—a fucking pencil—at the ready.

"It's kinda urgent. I work with Miller, this is about work, it's—"

The host interrupted, frazzled, eyes on the long line of pissed-off guests behind them. "If you don't have a reservation, you can wait outside until he's out of his meeting, and then if—"

Hattie seized voice control back. "Bitch, I'm Millions; I don't *do* reservations."

She launched herself past the host stand, weaving between four-tops and tray-laden bussers, toggling a squirt of adrenaline so she could outpace the poor woman chasing her. Hattie felt bad for her—guessing by the host's tan-lines, she was a recent hire from Earth, and almost certainly not paid enough to deal with difficult guests— whether they were tourists or Hattie.

"You can't—" the host called out.

But Hattie could, and did. Through the swinging doors, into the kitchen. The clatter of spoon against pot, the clean roar of a propane torch, the bounce of her feet on the rubber floor mat, the executive chef yelling as Hattie ran past the sauce station. This was Miller's

restaurant, enemy territory, yet it felt like home. Long
before the Millions had uploaded-and-copied themselves,
they'd worked in a molecular-gastronomy joint in
Chicago. The kitchen here was laid out exactly the same.
Had Miller done that on purpose? Either way, she was
recording everything. No way would she let all this juicy
intel on Miller go to waste.

"The fuck?" Miller flinched when she burst through
the door of his office. He sat behind an antique walnut
desk, surrounded by wall decor that resembled a dentist's
waiting room.

His body was a clone of the Millions' original body
from before they multi-instantiated themselves, before
they transitioned. Hattie didn't like looking at that fucking
body: all lanky limbs, bony and awkward, long ill-cared-
for hair, a rough dysphoria-denial beard, and clad in an
Earth-style merino business suit. He was the one who
stayed behind, who couldn't transition, who couldn't face
an endless digitized freedom. But that meant he was the
one who retained control over the Millions' earthside assets,
which he'd used to launch his first restaurant. Now here he
was, with a whole line of luxury restaurants, outcompeting
Hattie and fucking over his pet cheesemaker. Hattie had
no idea what Wayland saw in the man. The cheesemaker
was an enigma; she'd gone dark after the Crestfall debacle,
holed up in some remote station, producing the most
delicious fucking cheese Hattie had ever tasted. If only
Miller hadn't signed a deal to be her exclusive distributor.

"Millie?" he asked, using that hated nickname. "How did
you get here? You're supposed to be safe at the workshop
station. And *what* are you wearing?"

What a shady thing to say. But Hattie wasn't here
to settle her own score with Miller. She transferred full
body control over to Wayland, letting herself recede into
observer mode. She'd gotten the poor woman here, and
now she wanted to see the sparks fly.

"I saw what you did," Wayland said. "How *could* you? And you let me find out about it from the newsfeeds?"

Hattie winced. She had alerts set up for any news related to her main competitor, so she'd heard about the cheese cave immediately. Miller really was a fucker if he hadn't even warned her.

Miller's smile widened to expose perfect white teeth. Their first girlfriend—back on Earth, pre-transition—had loved those teeth. After Millions multi-instantiated, the poor woman had to deal with a steady stream of Millions copies independently deciding to try to reconnect with her. She'd blocked them all, and eventually the word had spread to not bother her anymore.

"You told me not to distract you from your cheese with—and I quote—unimportant business stuff."

"Oh and destroying my cheese-cave isn't important? You realize I use that for *making the cheese*, right?" Wayland strode up to Miller, trying to loom, clearly used to a body much taller than Hattie's short party-body. "Do you have any idea how long it took to—"

"Brilliant, isn't it?" he interrupted, pulling up a graph on his pad. "Remember how I set up that financial instrument to track the value of the cheese and allow me to sell fractional ownership shares?"

Hattie nearly screamed in delight. The drama! The intel! What a glorious night!

Miller pointed at the point where the line turned nearly vertical. "Well, look—this is what shares of RedOrion are going for."

Hattie was pissed; she was impressed. Miller was going to make *a lot* of money on this. She wanted to throttle the smarmy bastard.

"Augh, I don't care about your fucking financialization," Wayland said. "You killed the golden goose. The cave isn't just for storage. It took years to get the temperature and humidity just right, years to cultivate the exact ecology of mold and bacteria needed to develop the right flavors and textures. I thought you understood this? I can't make any more RedOrion—or any of the other lines—without the cave."

Miller waved her objections away. "I'll get you a new one. With the money I'm making, hollowing out an asteroid is a trivial expensive."

Wayland slammed her fist down on the desk and winced at the pain—clearly having forgotten she was wearing vulnerable flesh. "No! L3 is irreplaceable. Any asteroid you get me will start out sterile. With years of work, I could start making *new* cheeses, but they won't be the same. RedOrion, CometQuake, Herbed Death from Sirius—those lines will be gone, forever."

Tears blurred Hattie's view of Miller as she felt the full enormity of Wayland's grief and rage. Hattie reveled in it. She was furious too. Any slight against a fellow Millions was a slight against her. And Hattie had really fucking liked those cheeses.

Miller jumped up, excited. "Yes, that's the point! A completely inelastic supply curve means the price can only go up. Don't worry about your old lines. I evacuated L3, and moved all the cheese to an offsite vault. I've got *big* plans to expand our operations, and now I've got the funds to do it." He stood up, put a hand on Wayland's shoulder. Hattie wanted to pull away, but she'd ceded motor control to Wayland. "Think of this as a great opportunity to shake things up, to grow in a new direction. Isn't that what you Millions are all about?" An uncomfortable look flashed briefly across Miller's face before returning to manic optimism. "Think of it—fully automated production lines, with you as head of operations."

His eyes twinkled. Even Hattie had to admit this had always been the best part of her original self—the almost innocent excitement at whatever their latest fixation was.

Could she really hate the person she'd been? Well, yes, given he was an unctuous bastard whose latest fixation was stealing Wayland's cheese.

He squeezed their shoulder. "We should make an announcement! It's too bad you're wearing...whatever that is, but we can edit your real body in, or something."

That was too much for Hattie. What he'd done to Wayland was bad enough, but insulting her body? Her hard-won body, that she'd designed and birthed herself? His words were like a pinch of lithium dropped into the roiling waters of her anger.

Hattie grabbed voice control back, and screamed, "She just wants to make her cheese, you hairy fuck-wound!"

"Wha...?" Miller stumbled back, knocking over his chair, horror and disgust on his face. "Are there two of you in there?"

Hattie's answer was to grab him by the collar with her left arm, while her right arm hammered hard into his abdomen. He let out a panic-pained grunt and crumpled to the floor. She would cherish this memory forever.

Wayland seized voice control back. "I'm so sorry! Are you ok?"

Hattie could feel Wayland's panic. She ignored it, ignored Wayland requesting motor control back. She was too busy kicking Miller while he was down.

"Ah! Sorry! Stop it!" Wayland whined.

Hattie grabbed voice control back. "Shut up, Wayland. And you, Miller? You're even worse than I'd heard. I'm going to fucking ruin you for what you did to Wayland, you scraggly fucking phobic greed-sphincter."

Hattie gave him one last kick, then stomped out the door. She felt enough pity for Wayland that she gave her partial control, so she could cry her anxiety and grief out with their shared body. From the waist down, their body was an unstoppable force, a woman determined to split the world in twain to fit her will, charging out of the restaurant unrestrained. From the waist up, her body was a wreck of a woman, too deep in her own emotions to care about the cooks and servers and diners staring at her as she ran through the kitchen, through the front-of-house, out into the uncaring anonymity of the station concourse.

WAYLAND LET HERSELF feel the full weight of her grief. No more would she walk through the airlock into her cave, reveling in the cool and damp, breathing the heady scent of beneficial rot. Those microorganisms, so carefully cultivated, had felt like her children. She'd given them a home, given them cheese to feast on, and in return they became collaborators in her art. But Miller had condemned them to death, and now the place her skill and heart called a second home was beyond her reach.

Beyond Wayland's grief, beyond her anger at Miller, and her frustration with Hattie, what really stabbed her heart was the idea that this was *her* fault. If only she hadn't delegated so much to Miller. If only she hadn't been so hasty, had checked the Millions registry, had picked a different Millions to ask her favor. How many Millions were on the station right now? More than a hundred, surely. And she'd been lazy, and picked the worst possible choice: Hattie.

Weyland followed the chain of regret all the way back to Crestfall and the anti-austerity protests, then further to all the mistakes she'd made in the early years of multi-instantiated life, then the really old stuff from before she came out as trans. What a mess she'd been, when she didn't understand what was causing the wrongness that seemed to subsume the world. She'd been right to isolate in her workshop, to dissolve herself in the work. And now all that had been taken away.

When Wayland surfaced from her grief-reverie—her face flushed and nose snotty—she was sitting on a throne of myco-bricks, a glass of wine in her hands, surrounded by a lounging and feasting crowd of wildly clad people. They gazed at her with a mix of concern and adoration. Wayland blushed and looked down at her lap.

This was one of Hattie's Neo-Dionysian temple-diners. A wine-purple star-field fresco adorned the dome-shaped ceiling. The room was bright with grow lights to feed the modified grape vines that curled up the trellised walls. The floors were strewn with plush woven carpets, soft pillows, low tables laden with food and drink, and bodies either variously undressed or wearing the sort of clothes only understandable to orbital queer culture. The station ID'd about half the guests as Millions, the other half a smattering of other multi-instantiated lineages, initiated orbital-born singles, and adventurous visitors from Earth.

Wayland was largely unfamiliar with the Neo-Dio demi-religious revival. It had sprung up in the years after Wayland had sequestered herself in her workshop to avoid dealing with the aftermath of the Crestfall disaster. She felt uncomfortable seeing it all laid out in front of her; it reminded her too much of the early days of the Millions experiment when she—and all her copies—were filled with bubbly optimism. Back when she thought the ability to copy herself into unlimited variations of unlimited bodies would solve all her problems.

Hattie shunted Wayland into observer mode, wiped her tears away, took a long sip of wine, then stood, glass held high. The noise of the hundred-strong crowd quieted. "Siblings and cousins! Strangers and lovers! One of our own has been wronged. How many of us have enjoyed a creamy slice of RedOrion, full of the earthy bite of asteroid dust and the lusciousness of the love that made it?"

<What are you doing Hattie?> Wayland pinged on the internal feed. Hattie ignored her. The last thing Wayland needed was Hattie spilling the details of her embarrassing

failure to safeguard her cheese.

Hattie ignored her. "They said it was impossible to use orbital synth-milk to make cheese that could rival the quality of terrestrial cheese. Who proved them wrong? Millions Wayland!"

The crowd cheered. Hattie's wicked grin and the power of her voice egged them on. Wayland pinged Hattie again, <Please stop. This isn't helping, you've already made things bad enough. Remember what happened at the Titus Andronicus wrap party?> A low blow, reminding Hattie of a horribly embarrassing memory from their shared past. She felt Hattie's composure falter for a moment, a pause, a flinch, a tension in her chest and shoulders probably only perceptible to Wayland because she was inside Hattie's body.

Then Hattie straightened and continued. "Our reclusive cheesemaker, Millions Wayland, wronged by that villain Miller. Her beloved cheese stolen from her; the symphony of her craft-love ungraciously interrupted! She has toiled alone for too long."

The crowd chanted "Wayland! Wayland!"

"No more! *We* will be the instruments of her power. *We* will enact her revenge." Her arms wide, she motioned to the crowd. "Now, who wants to plan a heist?" The roar of the crowd overwhelmed all sound and sense.

<Fuck you,> Wayland messaged. Hattie grinned and descended into the noisome crowd, full of excited bodies that wanted to hug her, to comfort her, to share her anger, to help her. Why?! Surely these people hated her. She *deserved* to be hated after what she'd done. The five thousand unread messages blinking in her periphery were a testament to that. Wayland curled inward, the attention felt like a paring-knife rooting in an old scabrous wound.

She pulled open her internal emulation-systems control panel, selected the custom script labeled [disassociation] and clicked as fast as she could through all the informed consent warnings.

Peace through the elimination of self-awareness.

Her mind was empty. Not the lacuna of transmission, or the clamp-consumption of copying, this was the joyous emptiness of losing oneself in a good book, of sinking deep into a drunken bathtub, of emotional distress so huge it pushes away the feeling of being a body, free from the horror of a brain constantly thinking unbidden thoughts. It had been years and years since she'd needed to use this script. The revery-focus of cheesemaking had replaced all need for it—good because relying too much on the ability to ease the pain of consciousness was dangerous. She knew of several Millions who'd locked themselves in an endless cycle of entering synthetic dissociation, coming back to full consciousness, feeling the full weight of the pain that hadn't gone anywhere while they were under, then diving back into the soothing waters of self-elision. Over and over, with nothing to break the loop but outside assistance—which was often rejected.

Each Millions had to find their own reason to brave the rigors of existence. For Wayland, it was the cheese, but there was no synth-cream here, no basin or cheese-press. All she had was herself and a situation she couldn't see a way out of.

"Time to wake up, bitch," Hattie said to herself before kicking the cheesemaker out of her body. Wayland appeared next to her, translucent in emulation space, cringing against the soft light of Hattie's bedroom. Most of the room was taken up by an ostentatiously large bed, with the words *Business Expense* burned elegantly into the myco-plastic frame. What was left of the floor was covered in discarded clothes and empty biodegradable wine bottles. The neatly organized shelves contained

a wide array of sex toys (for the wide array of bodies
Hattie owned and had as guests) and a wild menagerie of
plush stuffed animals. She liked the mess of it; the clutter
reminded her that she'd made a nest here, and it would
take more to clean her out than a vacuum or a version of
herself willing to make deals with the devil.

"What the fuck, Wayland. You dipped out before the
party even got started." The poor girl had gone catatonic
like a victorian with the vapors. She'd missed all the best
parts, and worse, embarrassed Hattie, who'd spread the word
about the return of the cheesemaker. She was not in a mood
to be gentle. "I can't believe you used that awful dissociation
program again. You know that stuff is bad for you."

Wayland looked like she might cry, which meant she
was *really* upset. Emulation space flattened emotions; there
was nothing like a real body for feeling your feelings.

The cheesemaker's translucent simulated body was like
something from a synthetic-industrialist nightmare. Four huge
rubber hands at the end of four arms with bulging polymer
muscles. Impracticably tall, and with a face that clearly wasn't
built for expressiveness: slack cheeks, no eyebrows, a nose like
a cross between a butcher's cleaver and a star-nose mole, a
delicate mouth with soft-looking lips. It was terrifying; it was
hot. Hattie wondered what it would feel like to have those four
huge arms pin her to the bed, to kiss her fiercely, to use that
sharp mouth for more than tasting cheese.

"I wouldn't have had to fucking dissociate if you'd just
listened. I *told* you I didn't want a party—didn't want all
that attention. I am *grieving*. And a heist? *Really*?"

"Sounds fun, right? And how else are you going to
get your cheese back from that asshole?" Hattie could
think of several better ideas, but a heist was definitely the
most entertaining, and it had the delicious side effect of
financially ruining Miller. "If we seize the cheese, we can
use it as leverage to get Miller to return your asteroid to its
proper orbit."

"Can't we just hire someone to push the asteroid back into a safe orbit?"

"Did you have someone in mind?" As if, there was no way Wayland had the connections or resources for that. "No legit tug captain is going to agree to do it while Miller's title documents are validated by the trans-orbital court in Albuquerque. And even if you convince someone, good luck dealing with the ensuing legal shitstorm. You really want to get sanctioned by the whole station archipelago?"

Wayland started to object, but stopped short as Hattie pulled her dress over her head. Hattie liked the way the cheesemaker's eyes went wide, the way she looked at Hattie's perfect body. Yes, gaze at the wicked curve of hip to waist to shoulder, remember the feeling of those soft thighs rubbing together, of the glorious swell of that round belly. Hattie regretted kicking Wayland out of her body, but it was the fastest way to wake her up from dissociation.

Wayland looked away. If Wayland had been in an organic body, she'd surely be blushing. "I *planned* on hiring an ombudsperson. Once Miller calms down about the money stuff, I'm sure I can negotiate something reasonable."

Hattie gave her a skeptical look, then looped her finger into her panties and began pulling them off. Wayland was staring at the floor, but *surely* her peripheral vision was good enough to give her a glimpse of the way Hattie wiggled as she worked her underwear down her legs.

"He's not all bad. After Cr—" Wayland's voice broke. She seemed to shrink inward, flinching away from the memory. "Well, he's the one who set me up with a new workshop. He hollowed out L3 to be my cheese cave. I just need to remind him—"

Hattie threw her panties at Wayland. They sailed through her head, fuzzing her translucent body briefly. Wayland didn't flinch.

"Oh honey, he's using you. Whatever plan he has going on is clearly more important to him than you."

Wayland looked up, face still impassive, but anger clear in her voice. "Why do you even care? Where were you after, after—" her hands flailed. "After everything went sideways."

"You mean after *Crestfall*?" Hattie said the name that was now used more to signify the event than the station module that had been destroyed. She strode up to Wayland, put her face within kissing distance. "I *died* at Crestfall. The cops seized my body; I was running solely on the emulation servers you and your fucking copies destroyed. The only reason I'm alive now is because the Waverian Millions had a hidden backup."

"I...it wasn't me. We didn't want—"

"Shut up, Wayland. I don't give a shit about your excuses. I don't care *at all* what you did nineteen-fucking-years ago, whether it was on purpose or an accident. You're a Millions, you're in trouble, so I'm going to help you. It's as simple as that. If there's one thing we ought to have learned from Crestfall, it's that lack of solidarity will literally kill us. Which is why I'm going to heist your cheese back and then give you a new workshop, independent of Miller."

Wayland held silent. Hattie watched her, cursing that her cheesemaking-body was so impossible to read. Why did her fellow Millions always have to be so fucking stubborn and emotional?

"No," Wayland said, stepping back from Hattie. "A heist will just make things worse. I want to hire an ombudsperson. You already fucked my moral high ground when you assaulted Miller. Do you think *maybe* he's going to use that against us in negotiations?"

Hattie grinned, triumphant. As soon as Wayland said *us*, Hattie knew she was hooked. But, like a fish on the line, it might be better to let Wayland tire herself out before reeling her in.

"Fine," Hattie groan-sighed and flopped back onto her unmade bed. "We'll do it your way, the *boring* way, the way that will take *forever*, and won't actually achieve anything. Ungh." Then she sat up, all business, eyes sparkling. "I know a Millions we can use for this. Keep it in-house. Very professional; Miller will like her. Give me an hour to set everything up." She grinned. "And don't worry about the cost, I'll cover everything."

"Thank you. I..."

The poor woman sounded like she was about to start crying again. Hattie didn't have time to play therapist, right now she needed to get Wayland out the door while she set everything up. "Don't thank me until we get your cheese back. Why don't you go see the sights while I work on this? Lenaius has changed a lot in the last decade or two."

It only took a little more coaxing to get rid of Wayland. The truth was, Hattie did know a very impressive ombudswoman, but that wasn't what she needed right now. If Hattie let the negotiations succeed, her poor cheesemaker would fall right back under Miller's influence.

Unacceptable. Not only did Hattie want Wayland for herself, there was something *wrong* with Wayland— something beyond unresolved trauma about Crestfall, beyond being stuck in a workshop making cheese for nearly two decades. They'd shared a body—Wayland's brain emulation had run on Hattie's parietal emulation-implant—and it had almost *hurt* having Wayland in there with her. The way she moved, the way her emulated mind interfaced with the flesh neurons of her body, the way her thoughts seemed to sometimes jitter and sometimes stare into an empty hole. It reminded Hattie of nothing so much as dysphoria, that subtle invisible incomprehensible feeling of the wrongness of the world. When, so long ago, she'd learned the reason for that dysphoria-wrongness, it had been a revelation. But whatever was going on with Wayland wasn't anything related to gender.

Whatever Miller had done to Wayland, she couldn't let it continue. Her friend from the Waverian Millions copy-lineage might be able to help, but in the meantime, she needed negotiations to fail; she needed Wayland to come crawling back to her, desperate. And when a Millions needed a job done, the best person to turn to was herself. Time to thaw out a spare body, and ask her Waverian friend to hack the Millions registry again. Simple. The only missing piece was to make sure Miller was in peak asshole mode, but that wouldn't be hard.

THE STATION'S CENTRAL concourse was heavy with the crush of debarked tourists. They swirled around Wayland in their wool business suits, their plain unadorned bodies, their impractical-in-low-g dresses and dangly jewelry. It felt like she was back on Earth, in an airport or a shopping mall.

Nineteen years ago, this concourse had been full of fire, oily smoke suffocating anyone not lucky enough to have a too-scarce oxygen mask. She remembered the blood and fear, the screams and chants of desperate protestors on one side of the barricade, the silence of station security on the other.

It had started as an anti-austerity movement—protesting the rising price of Earth-made necessities—but had quickly transformed into a referendum on *the multi question,* as Earth called it. Multis were painted as dangerous, and when most nations on Earth ratified the One Person One Instance Treaty, station security had moved to seize Lenaius Station's emulation servers, located in Crestfall, one of the station's oldest modules.

Wayland's first cheese workshop had been on the wrong side of the barricade. Despite the station lockdown, she'd been able to reach it in emulation space, allowing her to watch in futile horror as station security set up a forward staging-area inside, trashing her carefully organized workspace. She screamed at them, wailed and struck with ethereal fists. They muted her, then smashed the hardpoint cameras, banishing her from her home.

The fate of her workshop had made it clear to Wayland what would happen if station security seized the emulation servers. Her fear had been a spur in her side, riding her towards desperate action. She'd copied herself nine times. Nine versions of herself, placed quickly in nine stolen bodies.

They abandoned the barricades, descended into the Crestfall module's utility systems, disabling structural interlocks, placing homemade explosive charges, and priming the module's long-dormant maneuvering thrusters. When everything was prepared, they hacked the module's environmental systems and activated a bogus decompression event, forcing a general evacuation of the module.

The plan had been to detach Crestfall, to push it beyond the reach of station security, to give the protestors time to regroup, time to survive just a little longer against the overwhelming power of Earth. But what happened instead became known as the Crestfall disaster.

Crestfall had been one of the first modules of Lenaius Station. Its connection to the rest of the station was complicated: legacy couplings, makeshift structural supports, a mess of wires and tubes and unlabeled systems. They'd done the best they could, working panic-fast against the clock, but they must have missed something. The decoupling—meant to be a clean excision—was instead like watching a novice badly butcher a chicken.

The fake decompression alert turned into a real one. The protective hull on both Crestfall and the remaining station tore like crepe-paper. And then, five minutes after decoupling, when Wayland was sure Crestfall was safely away despite the damage, the module exploded, killing the Nine Martyrs, destroying the emulation servers and the minds that lived in them, and murdering anyone who hadn't been able to evacuate.

Wayland should have died too, but one of the nine, Millions Nima, had betrayed her. She'd lured Wayland out of Crestfall, and then locked her in an airlock. "Tell them why we did it," Nima had said, voice crackling on the radio as Wayland screamed and pounded on the door.

Wayland survived, left to take the blame. Her messages filled with discourse and death wishes, conspiracy theories and legal threats. So many people—on Earth, and among the other multis—were convinced she'd destroyed Crestfall on purpose, or that she'd intended the module to impact Earth, killing millions. Anyone who tried to defend her quickly had the crowd turn on them as well.

Rather than face the tidal wave of hate, she'd hid.

Miller had found her, crying alone in a utility corridor. Instead of berating her, or offering words of comfort or absolution, he'd started talking endlessly about how much he loved her cheese. No mention of Crestfall, just creamline this and affinage that, for a full hour. From there, it was easy to fall into his orbit. All he ever wanted to talk about was her cheese, or his restaurateur ambitions. Those were safe topics for Wayland, things she could think about without her breath quickening, her hands trembling, her mind spiraling towards dissociation.

When he'd offered her a remote workshop in exchange for exclusive distribution rights, it felt like salvation. Miller was just like her, a Millions who'd been spurned by the others. He was the only one who appreciated what she'd sacrificed, and understood what she could offer the future. For two decades, she believed he was the only Millions she could trust. But now he'd betrayed her, and all those memories were tainted like a bad batch of cheese.

Lenaius Station felt similarly transformed. Now, the main concourse was clean. No trace of flame-scorch or blood-spatter. No ripped up floors, no barricades. And where was that little pharma-kiosk where the feathered man sold pills and patches? Now it was an Earth-based bank. Where was the tattoo and bodymod parlor that helped make her first plastiform body? Now it was a boutique selling luxury goods.

Wayland wondered if they'd actually won, or merely delayed the inevitable. Seeing how Lenaius had sanitized itself for the sake of commerce, could she really say the sacrifices her copy-children had made were worth it? And yet, for all the tourists and boutiques and banks, there were also temple-diners and emulation servers and Millions surviving and copying themselves.

Something familiar caught her eye in the luxury boutique's storefront. A stylized wooden club smashing a red wheel of cheese: the logo for RedOrion, her flagship cheese line. She floated into the shop, ignoring the frown of the clerk. Inside was a wild array of clothes that badly imitated station fashion, bric-à-brac that made her cringe with how it depicted a tourist-eye's view of station culture, and genuine asteroid fragments. It was unnerving to see the wild and diverse culture of the station archipelago sanitized and packaged for the convenience of tourists.

In the back of the boutique, in a small refrigerated section, was a display with her cheese. Only a few of the palm-sized plastic-wrapped wheels remained. She reached out to touch one, but emulation space gave her only the vaguest sensation of pressure, nothing like the wealth of information provided by a flesh fingertip or the mechanoreceptors of her work-body. She considered buying a copy, just to taste—one last time—the way the red brine-washed rind transitioned gradually to the nutty salty funky cream within.

The price tag—scrawled over with a number much higher than the already far-too-expensive original price—stopped her. Who could afford this? Not her, or anyone else she knew. When she'd first started making cheese in her tiny apartment kitchen, she would give the cheese away.

A truckle here for a friend's party, three truckles for the quintet that ran the synth-milk bioreactor, a barrel of whey to the recycler's guild. None of that cheese had been particularly good. She'd been new to the craft and had to work in her awful cramped apartment kitchen. Worse, synth-milk back then was something hastily cooked up in shoddy bioreactors. It lacked the full breadth of oligosaccharides, fatty esters, casein and whey proteins, and all the other subtle molecules that combined to form the terroir of real animal milk. Even so, that awful cheese had been station-made, and thus an inexpensive luxury for people used to only eating the small range of foods amenable to being grown in aquaponics rigs or produced in bioreactors.

Now, her cheese was being sold in the types of places inaccessible to most stationers. How had that happened? She'd trusted Miller to handle the business side of things, and while she'd known that he was the arch-assimilationist among the Millions (if he even counted as a Millions), she though he shared her goal to enrich the gustatory ecosystem of the station archipelago, to better allow *everyone* who lived in space to have access to high quality food. To show it was possible to create a delicious and sustainable cycle: recycler nutrient-glop synthesized into milk, milk turned into cheese, cheese eaten and turned into shit, shit recycled into nutrient-glop, and so on. No more burning fuel to bring cheese up from Earth.

But now, he'd betrayed her, betrayed everything she'd worked for. And for what? To chase the favor of terrestrial financial markets? It seemed pointless...unless he thought he could buy amnesty and return to Earth. The thought chilled Wayland. As angry as she was at Miller right now, she'd grown used to relying on him. If he fled down the gravity well and returned to Earth, she'd have no recourse against him. She'd be all alone. Would he really leave her?

And if she couldn't trust Miller, was Hattie any better?

When she'd approached Hattie, she thought she'd just
be borrowing a body, quick and impersonal, and then
back to cheesemaking. Every minute she spent with this
tempestuous other version of herself, she felt like she was
sinking into the quicksand of the other woman's plans
and desires. Not to mention racking up Unique Life
Experiences that would make reintegration with her self
back at the workshop difficult or impossible.

But who else could she turn to? Every moment, her cheese
cave hurtled closer to the sun, every moment, more of her
precious cheese was sold to those who didn't appreciate the
purpose for which she'd made it. She was at the mercy of
Hattie, who was willing to pay for an ombudsperson. She
was at the mercy of Miller's willingness to negotiate. The
only way forward was to trust her other selves—and hope.

MILLER WAS SURPRISED at the choice of venue for the
meeting with Wayland and the ombudsperson. The cafe—
known for its zero-g wraps—ranging from refried beans
and cheese, to spicy dried-banana and peanut-butter—had
some of the worst food on the station. But at least that
meant it was mostly empty.

Wayland and the ombudsperson were already there,
sitting close together around a plastic table, heads almost
close enough to touch, whispering furiously. He hadn't
wanted to involve an ombudsperson, but Wayland insisted.
At least this copy of himself—named Millions Emma—had
impeccable credentials, legitimate accreditation on Earth,
and absolutely no known entanglements with Hattie.

Best of all, her body looked normal. Short and thin, with
long silver-gray braided hair, a small button nose, and a calm
business-like look on her face. Exactly the sort of person
you'd encounter at a law firm or bank. Safe and reliable.

Miller stumbled when he recognized the body Wayland was wearing: Hattie's business body. Fuck, he hated that body. He hated the curve of its smirk when Hattie blocked his expansion permits at inter-module planning-council meetings. He hated the arrogant sway of its wide hips, the ostentatious shimmer-tattoos and the way its soft roundness seemed to mock him by saying *I'm enjoying my life, why aren't you?*

Worse, if Wayland was wearing *that* body, it meant she was working with Hattie—and that he'd been right to suspect Hattie was the copy who'd been riding with Wayland when she assaulted him. And clearly Hattie *wanted* Miller to know that. Surely the universe was conspiring against him. Of all the people Miller did not want getting involved in this extremely delicate situation, Hattie was at the top of the list.

"Hey." Miller plopped down into the empty seat beside Wayland. "*She's* not in there, is she? You came alone?"

Wayland smiled. "Just me, thank goodness. She's a lot isn't she."

Miller recoiled. To see Wayland's tentative smile rendered on *that* face was horrific. If the cheesemaker was already wrapped up in Hattie's scheming, he'd have to completely reconsider his plans for this meeting. First, regain composure. Then, attack. Keep them off balance.

"Cool," he said, and pretended his grimace was for the menu he held in his hands. "Are you going to apologize?"

"It wasn't me! I tried—"

Emma cut in. "First we need to set some ground rules for—"

"I don't want this to jeopardize your work," Miller interrupted them both. "Or, our relationship. But," he paused, gave them both a long look, daring them to cut him off. "I'm willing to drop all charges *if* you agree I own the remaining cheese, *and* you promise not to reintegrate with your copy back at the workshop, *and* both Hattie and this Wayland copy sign a DNI agreement."

DNI: *Do Not Interact.* It would bar Wayland from messaging Miller or seeing him in emulation space. And if she circumvented the agreement with physical bodies, then the Lenaius inter-module council—and all other stations with mutual jurisdiction treaties—would enact harsh sanctions against her.

Emma frowned. "That's not the demand you messaged me about before this meeting. Are you—"

"First off," Wayland interrupted. "I wasn't the one who punched you—"

"—and kicked me. I have it on camera."

Wayland slammed her palm on the table. Good. He needed to goad her into fury for this to work. "It wasn't me! If we pull the logs from Hattie's motor cortex, it will clearly show it was Hattie who performed any assault that might've happened."

Miller did a little victory dance in his head. A recorded confession—or at least enough of one to get the station council to pull Hattie's body-logs—was an unexpected boon. Now he just needed to seal the deal.

"You both need to calm down," Emma said. "And Miller, it's entirely unacceptable for you to bait-and-switch your demands."

Miller was souring rapidly on this ombudsperson. Her pseudo-saccharine smile reminded him too much of Hattie. Was that unfair? They were the same person after all—literally all of them were just copies of him, running around causing trouble, ruining his reputation, then leaving him to clean up their messes.

"Fine, it wasn't you," he said, ignoring Emma. "If you're willing to testify against Hattie here in Lenaius, *and* in the trans-orbital court at Albuquerque, then we can forget this incident ever happened and go back to how things were." He grabbed Wayland's half-eaten wrap, took a bite, and immediately regretted his decision. The beans were undercooked—dry and hard, with an unpleasant soapy aftertaste. The thick mayo didn't help.

"Back to how things were? You'll save my cheese cave?" Wayland asked, as Miller coughed up the food into a napkin. The way she looked at him, her big brown eyes flush with hope and fear, was almost enough to melt his heart, even if it was bizarre seeing that expression on a face that was usually mocking him.

"Look," he said. "I know you're mad. I get that. I should've explained everything to you, shouldn't have let you find out about it from the newsfeed." He pulled his hand down across his face, feeling his skin stretch. "I've just been so busy. I'm...I'm sorry, Wayland." His regret was genuine—he'd been too caught up in his desperation to make enough money to deal with his Earthside legal entanglements. He'd thought Wayland would remain safe and productive in her workshop, free from outside interference. To have a copy of her show up here on Lenaius and become entangled with Hattie was a terrifying disaster. "But I'm sorry, I can't bring back L3. I'm waaay over-leveraged on this whole thing. It would *ruin* me if we screw around with investor expectations. I'm sorry, but those cheese lines have to die."

Wayland's borrowed face fell—so expressive compared to her work-body.

Emma cut in, "So this is only about the money for you? Is there a price you can name for saving Wayland's cheese?" Emma tapped on the floor. "These bulkheads feel solid, but remember, we're in space. We all know financial ledgers are useless when the air and the food run out."

"I know that!" Miller shouted. Weren't ombudspeople supposed to be neutral? Why did it feel like this one was entirely on Wayland's side? "I'm doing this for you. For us. You've been locked up in your workshop so long, you haven't seen how the tide has turned." He leaned in close, lowering his voice. "After what you did during Crestfall, Earth pulled back. But we all knew that was temporary."

Wayland flinched, looked down at her hands. "It wasn't me," she whispered.

He ignored her. Crestfall wasn't the point; he didn't need her getting sidetracked by guilt. "Any autonomy you won here was always going to be temporary. It's been nineteen years. They see us prospering up here, and they want in. And not just on the tourism and industry side of things. You lot are sitting on a goldmine of intellectual property and cognitive data. You think they're going to leave you be?" Miller paused and debated telling Wayland about the lawsuit, and the threat to all the Millions. But he couldn't afford to let Hattie find out. She'd almost certainly turn this delicate situation—which he was handling—into a complete clusterfuck, or use it against him to enact petty revenge, dooming them all. Better to keep things vague with this Wayland-copy, distract her with a different threat. "They've already started re-asserting control in a million small ways. Did you know the Americans have begun arming their ships up here?" He pointed a finger-gun at her. "There's a railgun aimed at your head right now. You, uh, didn't hear that from me."

"But the treaty..." Wayland trailed off, her face a map of shock.

It was good that she was afraid. The long-term implications were terrifying. "Your little cooperatives and temple-diners are no match for what's coming. What do you think will happen if the Americans get control of your emulation servers? If we want to stay in power, we can't rely on riots or mutual aid or whatever weird pseudo-religious nonsense those Neo-Dionysians get up to. Someone needs to be the adult in the room. Money is the only type of power we have access to that they'll actually respect. And we're going to need a lot of it if we want to survive."

"Who is *we*?" Wayland asked.

The question shocked Miller. He thought he had Wayland under control. The idea that she was doubting him was troubling. Was this entirely Hattie's influence? Or did the rot extend to the original Wayland?

Miller patted her shoulder, putting as much condescension in the gesture as he could. She flinched; good. "Really? You think I'd let them deactivate all the copies you made of me?" She was right to be afraid of that scenario. Emulation tech was highly regulated on Earth, and most nations had ratified the One Person One Instance treaty, tightly controlling what could be done with copies. "I don't want that any more than you do. But there have to be limits. The more normal you can be, the more you can assimilate into proper society, the less they'll want to eliminate you."

"I think we've gotten off topic," Emma frowned at both of them.

"Oh, I almost forgot, one last thing," Miller interrupted, again. Wayland looked like she was actually considering his point of view, which was *not* what he wanted at this point. This Wayland-copy was irretrievably corrupted—she'd been running on hardware supplied by Hattie and thus could never be trusted again. He needed her angry enough to reject any offer of compromise. If he made it look like it was her fault the negotiations failed, he might have an easier time getting other Millions lineages to fall in line. "In addition to the DNI, I want this Wayland-copy to sign a non-compete with the original back at the workshop."

"Absolutely fucking not," Wayland said, her face flushed.

The one advantage of having Wayland inhabiting the worst body on the station was that he knew—or at least suspected—the body had its emotional valence cranked up to eleven. Was her eye twitching?

"Are you fucking damaged? You really think I'd ever agree to give up cheesemaking? The one thing that saved me after..." Her voice cracked. She stood abruptly. "Fuck you."

Bingo. Miller's grin curled the edge of his lips. Time to seal the deal. "You could still make cheese, just not sell it—or give it away. No using 'mutual-aid' or whatever to circumvent the agreement."

Wayland stood there, mouth moving, but no words coming out, her hands clenching and releasing. He almost felt bad for her. Even if copies of him were dime a dozen—far too many of them for his tastes—he didn't like causing emotional pain to a living breathing person. He had to remind himself that this Wayland copy was corrupted, that what mattered was the one back at the workshop, and the future only *he* could secure for his misguided copies.

He glanced at the ombudsperson. Weird that she wasn't jumping in to try to salvage the negotiations. Emma sat there, absorbed in her pad. Was she on a call? She looked up at him, feeling his gaze, and grinned a wild grin that he was used to seeing on Hattie just before she fucked him over. He scrambled to double-check the Millions registry ID pinned to her cognitive runtime. It said the same thing as before. Millions Emma, accredited ombudsperson, same bland lineage, no overt connection to Hattie. What the fuck was going on here?

He stood, looked down at Wayland who was still sputtering for words. "You have no idea what I've been protecting you from. If only you'd been a little more patient and come to me first." He turned and began to walk away, stopped, shouted over his shoulder. "One last piece of advice? Be more careful who you make friends with. Not all of my copies are as trustworthy as you."

He'd assumed she'd learned that lesson the hard way during Crestfall. It didn't matter; this Wayland was a sunk cost. Far more concerning was the implication of someone having compromised the Millions registry. He needed to talk to that bastard, Ensign Homme. Fuck, this day just couldn't get any worse.

"Goodnight, sweet thing," Hattie said to herself as she

activated the autopilot on the Emma-body and told it to go back to its cryobay. She slipped into emulation space and went to find Wayland, who'd run off crying in her borrowed body.

The negotiations had gone even better than Hattie had hoped. Her deception hadn't even been necessary; even a real ombudsperson couldn't have salvaged *that* mess. Miller wasn't a savvy operator at the best of times, but he wouldn't make things such a trainwreck unless he was doing it on purpose. What was that asshole up to?

Hattie found Wayland on a bench in the crowded concourse, face puffy, the shoulders of her blouse dotted translucent with tears. Hattie slipped into the body—no permissions needed, it was registered to her—and said with their shared lips, "So...? How'd it go?"

"Fuck you. Your ombud was useless."

"That's surprising." Hattie grabbed motor control, stood, and started walking to the temple-diner. "I've used her before. She's quite good actually—when she has reasonable people to work with. I think the real problem here is that you trusted Miller."

"He didn't use to be like that, I swear. And if you can't trust yourself..." Wayland repeated the first half of that old joke. What an ironic thing for *this* particular copy to say. But the poor girl had been through enough, and didn't deserve a lecture about how Miller only barely counted as *yourself*. His claim to being the original was laughable—even if it was true that he'd diverged from the trunk line of Millions copies way back at the beginning.

Their actual original body had died as part of the initial multi-instantiation upload, which required the brain to be removed from the body and then turned translucent via the removal of all lipids. This allowed the brain's full connectome to be scanned—avoiding the cell damage caused by earlier methods that required cutting tissues into thin slices.

Miller was one of the three copies that had resulted from that bootleg experiment—done with stolen intellectual property from a biotech startup that had gone bankrupt after authorities on Earth learned how the tech was being used in orbit.

For reasons known only to him, Miller had a full blown panic attack three months after instantiation, thawed out the corpse of the real original, and ran off with it. Years later, he'd shown up on Earth, claiming he was the real Miller, and used his credentials to steal all the copies' assets on Earth. The idea that he'd *ever* been trustworthy was absurd. Did Wayland not remember this? Had Miller tinkered with her memory or her judgment? Or had she just been hands-deep in a fucking curd bath for too long?

They entered the temple-diner and several guests cheered. Hattie waved them off. There would be time for that later. For now she needed to handle Wayland.

When they were safe in Hattie's bedroom, she sat on her bed, wiped away Wayland's tears, and asked, "So, is the heist back on?"

"Was it ever off?" Wayland's voice was suspicious. "Or were you planning to do it regardless of how negotiations went? And why are you even helping me so much? Don't you have your temple-diners to run?"

Shit, what had tipped Wayland off? Hattie needed to redirect the cheesemaker, so she smirked, and cupped their cheek, drawing her fingers along their jawline. "You have no idea who you are, do you? Among my lineage, my copy-mothers and copy-children, you are a *legend*. A reclusive genius, your artistry sublime, your skill unmatched. You were one of the first who proved a multi could be successful, could be *the best* at something. Do you know how many Millions look up to you? How many model themselves after you? Do you not read your messages?"

Hattie felt their body flush with heat, though whether that was from her own admiration for Wayland—pretty

much every Millions shared the original's competence-
kink—or Wayland's response to praise, she couldn't say. "I...
asked Miller to handle all my mail. After, uh, Crestfall,"
Wayland gulped, saying the word. "My messages were full
of abuse, death wishes. From stationers, Earthers, and
even Millions."

"Oh you poor thing, you didn't deserve any of that."
Hattie hugged their body tight, the sensory sharing
making it feel simultaneously like she was hugging herself
and another person who just happened to have the exact
same body. "And fuck Miller. I'm sure he just loves
soaking up all the praise you deserve. If there's one bad
thing people say about you these days, it's that you run
with that dirt-loving asshole."

"Do they still talk about...what happened?"

Hattie ignored the question. After her resuscitation,
the Waverian Millions had imposed a strict condition:
do not poke the bear. Do not investigate Crestfall; don't
discourse about it; don't even think about it. They wanted
the community to move on, to focus on building the
future instead of hurting each other over the past. Plenty
of Millions—those who'd survived Crestfall, who hadn't
needed to be restored from a secret Waverian backup—
didn't agree with the Waverian commandment for silence.
They still argued about it on social feeds, and by now had
formed into two camps: those who thought the backlash
against the Crestfall instigators was justified, and those who
thought the backlash was worse than the actual event itself.
One advantage of having literally died during Crestfall was
it gave Hattie an excuse for not getting involved.

But poor Wayland had no such protection from the
horror of whatever had happened that day. Hattie wanted
so badly to keep holding her tight, to protect her from
the past and her fears for the future. Wayland needed her
help, and Hattie needed Wayland. "If there's an upside
to this tragedy, it's that Miller's not going to be the one to

benefit from your skill anymore. You'll need a new patron. And a new body." Hattie pressed her thighs together, arched her back. "Please let me order you one. I want to kiss you so bad."

Hattie felt the heat of her desire, a glowing line from chest to groin. Wayland, still sharing their body, must feel it too. Hattie pulled up the body control panel, and did the equivalent of pushing her up against a wall by keying them both more deeply into the sensations of their shared body. She was suddenly very aware of her own breath, growing faster and shorter; the feeling of nipples hardening against the softness of her bra; the way her wide belly pushed out against the tight fabric of her blouse; the quickening pulse of her heartbeat, throbbing in her chest, neck, and groin.

Wayland flailed, hands shaking. Hattie cursed herself for going too fast. She needed to slow down, dial back their body's sensorial intensity, and ask Wayland's permission.

"Is this ok?" Hattie asked.

Wayland gasped for air. The deluge of sensory stimulation had receded momentarily, but she still felt like she was drowning. *Was* it ok? Was anything?

Her work had been her foundation, a solid surface built over decades. Now it was all crumbling beneath her. Her cheese and cave were gone; Miller had betrayed her; and the woman she'd turned to—the only ally she had left—wanted to fuck her.

Wayland debated jumping back into the cool waters of emulation space. This wasn't what she came for; it had been a long time since she'd done anything like this. Her body—Hattie's body—felt like a piano wire, struck and resonating with shared desire. She could—if she wanted—dive deeper into that resonance, lose herself in the delicate dance of switching who controlled which muscles, who felt the fullness of their sex organs—hands, dick, cunt, breast, mouth—and how far to dissolve the border between *me* and *you*.

Should she?

She'd known this woman for barely more than a day; she'd known her for most of their original life. Which weighed more, their shared years growing up, or the ways they'd diverged since splitting?

And what of Wayland back at the workshop? If the two Waylands hadn't already accrued too many Unique Life Experiences to reintegrate together, then surely *this* would push her far past that point. Wouldn't it just be easier to go back, let herself be subsumed into the font from which she had sprung, return to the glories of cheesemaking? But could she dare face her other self, knowing she had failed here on Lenaius, that her cheese and cave still hurtled towards the all-consuming sun?

Wayland sighed, half from desire to give in, half from desire to not want this so badly. But she *did* want it, needed to feel like she wasn't alone, like she might matter fiercely to at least one other person. She needed a distraction from the five-thousand unread messages winking in her periphery. She bit her lip—their lip. "Show me what this body can do."

Hattie gently took motor-control, moving their hands around the wide curve of their belly, feeling the way the skin and fat gave way to the muscle and bone of her hands. Then, one hand went up to a breast, the other down to their groin. It'd been so long since Wayland had lived in a flesh body. The softness and the slick shift of flesh on flesh overwhelmed her. The sensations of the station—the constant vibrations and smells and clangs— were washed away by the tides of a body moving to its own desires.

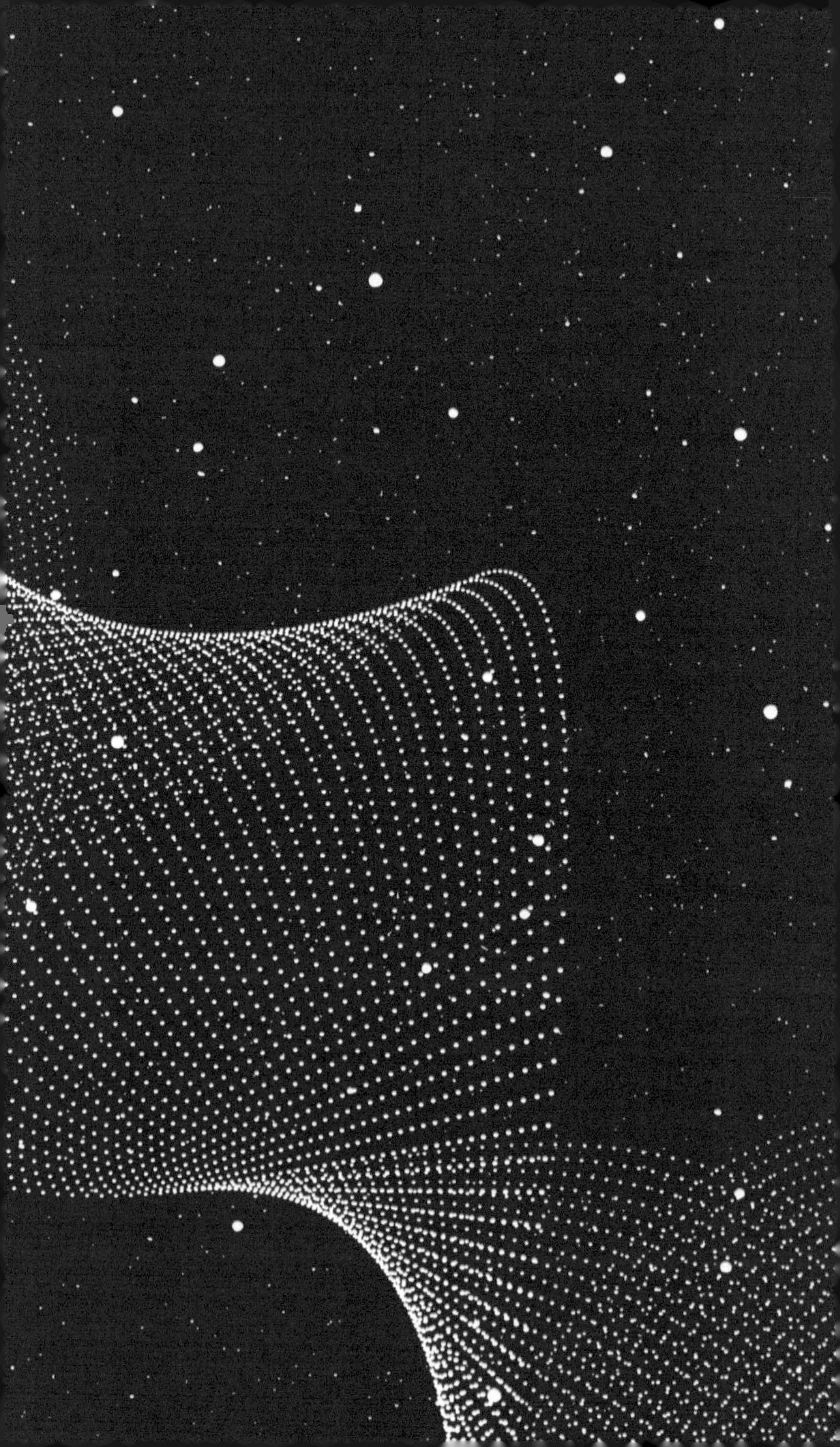

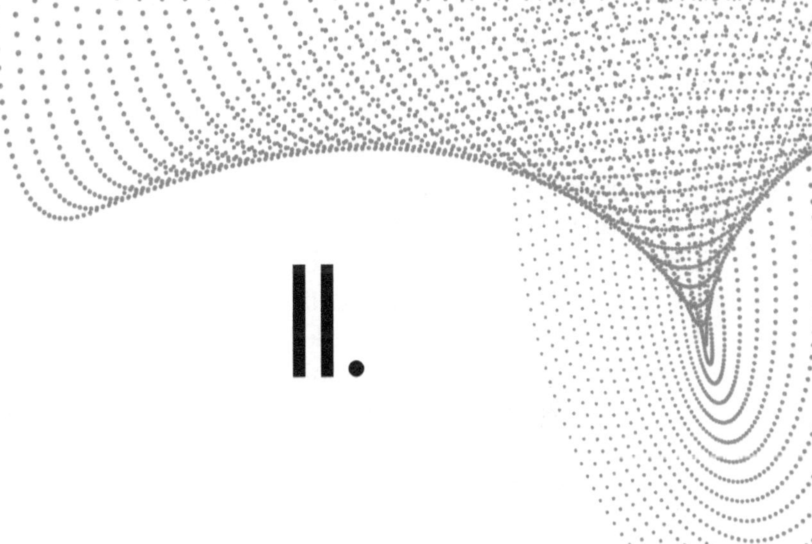

II.

N**EVER LET YOUR** adversary see your fear. That was one of Miller's guiding principles. Fear was weakness; vulnerability was a lever, and with the right lever, his opponents could move the world against him. So before he met with Ensign Homme, he armored himself with his best suit, and took a little mauve pill to keep his nerves down.

Pills were safe, he told himself as he swallowed it. These ones came from a reputable pharma vendor. He knew exactly what was in them; he knew exactly how they'd interact with the complexities of his endocrine system and his flesh brain. The Millions were fucking fools to let their thoughts run on computers—unreliable, untrustworthy, unstable.

Ensign Homme's vault was in a warehouse down at one end of Lenaius Station's central utility spire. Getting there meant sharing a service elevator with an assortment of workers wearing grease-smeared synthetic bodies. They stared at him in his suit; he stared at the elevator's display-panel, counting down the levels to the vault. Anything to avoid seeing the writhing utili-tentacles the worker next to him sported instead of hands.

He didn't belong here down at the base of the station. Stepping off the elevator into the heat of the empty hallway was relief, its aluminum walls scuffed with grime, the insulation tattered, the row of airlock doors evenly spaced like coffins. Each one led to a miniature private warehouse with an integrated docking port, so ships could unload their cargo directly.

There was nothing remarkable about the airlock door before him, nothing to differentiate it from the others except *Unit W113-S: Private Use, No Entry Permitted* stenciled roughly in crimson. He paused, took a breath. Had the medicine kicked in? Yes? His thoughts felt smooth like aioli, his heartbeat regular as the rocking chop of a chef's knife. Everything was going to be just fine.

The airlock opened; he stepped in. Two men wearing US Space Force fatigues pointed vacuum-rated guns at him, while a third frisked him roughly, first with his hands and then with a multi-scanner. Despite the medicine, he felt every twitch of the guns deep in his gut, like he was a marionette and his strings were attached to the death-speaking gun barrels. Nobody was supposed to have guns on Lenaius, but the station council didn't know, and even if they did, what could they do? They didn't have guns.

"You know," Miller said, attempting—and failing—at nonchalance, "I come here at least once a week. You know who I am, you can see me coming on the cameras in the hallway. So why so twitchy with those guns? What happens if you accidentally blow my head off?

I'm not a fucking multi, I've only got the one body."

The soldier who was searching him jammed the scanner against his neck. "Protocol, sir." He had a thick Boston accent, but his head was obscured by the armor's faceplate. Miller had no idea if it was the same guy as last time. "It could be anyone inside your meat. You know how the multis are. I wouldn't put it past 'em to rip your head open, stuff one of themselves inside, then rig the body with those blades that pop out of the hands, or maybe a skullgun."

"That's not..." Miller started, but gave up on the idea of explaining that while the Millions were perverted, they weren't into skullguns or handblades, and they certainly didn't need to rip anyone's head open.

One of the gun-wielding soldiers chimed in. "You know, you might not even realize it'd been done to you. Buddy of mine in a private outfit got pop-fucked by a p-zomb with a fuckin' extendo-tongue-sword. I saw it on vid. Tongue shot out, wrapped round his neck, snnkk'd his head right off."

"I don't...know what any of that means," Miller replied, as the other soldier roughly investigated his inner thigh. It felt like these security checks got more invasive each time.

The third soldier rolled his eyes. "You're all clear, sir. Ensign Homme is waiting in the foreman's office."

Miller practically leapt out of the airlock. The warehouse floor was a maze of server racks, full of the deafening roar of cooling fans. LEDs winked furiously as the computers performed their tasks. It always reminded Miller of a nightmare he once had involving Christmas decorations come to life.

The foreman's office had been cleared of all furniture to accommodate a massive holo-display. Ensign Homme paced around it, his eyes wild. He was short, with a buzzcut and a face that reminded Miller of guys with sunglasses-in-a-car selfie profile pics that would send him *hey* messages back before he'd detransitioned. Homme's polo shirt and khaki pants looked like they'd fit in better on a golf-course than a clandestine operations center on a space-station. Before Homme had joined the military by buying an officer's commission, he'd been the VP for Strategic Global Acquisitions at a consulting firm specializing in leveraged buyouts. Miller had no idea what was going on down on Earth that this was a desirable career path.

"The fuck are you doing here, Miller?" Homme said as he clicked off the holo-display. Not that Miller had implants that could record his glimpse of the multi-dimensional analysis diagram, or the skills to analyze it.

"I think someone's hacked the Million's registry. I thought you might be interested—or might be able to help."

"So fucking what? This whole station's security is swiss-fucking-cheese. I've got my worms so deep up this station's asshole that—" Homme paused, peered hard at Miller with eyes like paring knives. "Is this about your cheesemaker AI? I've got reports saying it's loose on the station."

Miller shifted foot to foot. Hard to remain impassive with those eyes on him. "The original, uh, AI is still secure in the workshop, still making cheese. So we're good there." Miller wasn't going to quibble with Homme about whether original-Wayland was an artificial intelligence. Technically, she was still a person, a copy of a human brain. But she was running on hardware that optimized her thoughts, helped her focus solely on the cheesemaking to the exclusion of all else. He'd isolated her in a remote asteroid work-station partly to keep outside parameters from distracting or influencing her, and partly to protect her from Homme and his Earthside handlers. They were desperate for the tech to manufacture human-derived intelligences, like Wayland but more extreme. It would revolutionize information technology, they said. Imagine a personal assistant as smart and adaptable as a real human, infinitely copyable, fully owned and controlled by a company. Wayland was Miller's last bargaining chip, and he'd been able to keep her safe in the workshop until now.

Homme grimaced. "Good, because I do not give a single fucking ratshit about this heist drama you've stirred up—so long as your payments are on time and it doesn't fuck with operational security down here."

"Heist?" Miller hadn't heard anything about a heist.

Homme sighed. "You really are the dumbest motherfucker on this station. Your rival Hattie is working with the AI to steal your cheese. Did you really not know? She was fucking bragging about it in front of her whole whorehouse restaurant. I fucking hate it up here."

"Shit. Shit, shit. Can you do something?" Why did it always feel like Hattie was two steps ahead of him? If she stole the cheese back, she'd ruin everything; she'd doom him and all the Millions with him.

"Fuck no, I'm not going to help. Didn't I just tell you that? I am here to do exactly two things, and one of those is enforcing the court order against you. And if you fuck up? If you miss your payments? I will be more than happy to fulfill the original, more punitive, terms. I have *orders.* Do you understand?"

Miller nodded. How stupid had he been to think Homme would bother helping him? Between his exhaustion and the stress, he wasn't thinking straight. He was so tired, hadn't slept well in weeks due to a combination of workload and anxiety about his legal troubles. Not to mention anger at how the Millions treated him. This was entirely their fault. If they'd kept their heads down, if they'd avoided attracting Earth's attention, none of this would've happened. But no, they had to make waves with their protests and their screeds and the whole Crestfall disaster. Now, everyone on Earth knew about multi-instantiation and those with an eye for profit understood what an opportunity the technology was.

He'd been stupid to upload himself all those years ago. He'd been so arrogant, he thought he could get away with it. Surely the little biotech startup that had patented the tech wouldn't come after him for intellectual property violations, not in orbit. And for a while, he'd been right. But five years ago, a private equity firm had bought the bankrupt remains of that startup, and now they were coming for Miller and all the Millions, claiming not just patent infringement, but that their existence violated the company's trade secrets. And of course Miller was the one they served with papers. He was the only real legal entity according to the trans-orbital courts. This was his burden to bear alone, which was probably a good thing because if the other Millions found out, their 'help' would surely make things worse—or they'd use it against him. He'd been tempted to tell Wayland, just to have a sympathetic ear, but he knew better than to distract her with a crisis she wasn't equipped to handle. So yes, he'd gutted the golden goose, as Wayland accused, but how else was he supposed to raise enough money to pay off a private equity firm powerful enough to get the actual US military to enforce their intellectual property?

Miller decided to cut his losses. He handed Homme the wheel of cheese he'd brought. It was dark green beneath the plastic wrap—Herbed Death from Sirius, Miller's least favorite of Wayland's cheeses. Yet now this single wheel was worth an obscene amount of money.

Homme grabbed the wheel and dragged it under his nose, snorting the redolent smell of dill. "And the certificate?"

"Of course." Miller fished the memstick with the digitally signed ownership certificate out of his pocket. When Homme reached out for it, he jerked it back. "My settlement with the court is mutually binding. You'll get your cheese, and I'll make sure the cheese is worth its weight in gold. And you are going to stay down here in your vault and not let whatever other operations you've got going on—don't deny it, you wouldn't have this whole setup if you weren't up to something—you won't let all that interfere with any of *my* business."

Homme's face was impassive. "I solemnly swear I have zero interest in high-end dining establishments. Enough chitchat. You're dismissed." Homme waved him towards the door.

Homme's threats, the laughter of the soldiers, the whir of the fans cooling the servers, all echoed in Miller's ears as he headed back up to his office. Just once, he would like some appreciation for the sacrifices he made.

"Is this...the best you can do?" Wayland asked, upon seeing the new body Hattie had procured for her. She didn't want to be ungrateful, but this was obviously just a utili-skeleton modified to resemble her old work body. It had clearly lived a long life as a rental unit, seeing abuse from people who knew it was just a temporary body, shed as easily as a dirty outfit at the end of the day. The plastic was scuffed and the joints worn. It only had two arms, instead of the four Wayland had grown used to. Worse, when she hopped in, she could immediately tell the left arm proprioception was misaligned, and the right knee seized up when she tried to kneel. Nothing that would create serious motor control issues, but enough to cause occasional clumsiness and distract her brain with an uneasy smear of background dysmorphia.

For all that, it felt more like home—more like her beloved work-body—than emulation or Hattie's body. Over the years of her work, she'd grown to love the precision of digital nerves and sensors; the way piezo-rubber muscles could hold a position indefinitely without concern for the painful buildup of lactic acid; the ability to script a set of motions—like stirring a water bath—allowing her primary cognition threads to focus entirely on the high-level needs of her work.

Even better, this utili-skeleton lacked an endocrine system with which to betray her. She could watch the way Hattie's hips moved side to side without feeling a rush of heat from sternum to groin; she could feel Hattie's hand on her waist without her knees losing all structural integrity. That made it much easier to struggle with her brain spooling out fantasies or memories of Hattie's body, her wicked grin, the curve of—

Execute dissociation script: fifteen-hundred milliseconds. Thought; interrupted. Void-cool relief. Resumption; full cognition.

Hattie cocked her head. Had she noticed the brief blip of Wayland's absence? "You alright?"

"I'm, uh, fine." Wayland pretended she was practicing arm movements, getting used to the new body. It was similar enough to her old four-limbed body that she kept trying to move a second set of arms that weren't there, or pass tools or bowls to hands that didn't exist.

Hattie slid her hand along the contours of Wayland's bicep, gently squeezing the firm piezo-rubber muscles. "Great, because there's something I need you to do before we can start planning the heist."

THERE WAS ALMOST nothing Wayland wanted less than to get involved with this Neo-Dionysian nonsense. But Hattie had insisted that Wayland needed to be initiated into the secret rites. She'd argued, of course, but what use were feeble words against the force of Hattie's personality and the fact that she had the resources Wayland needed?

Which is why she found herself sitting naked in a wine-purple pseudo-flesh body on a wide table, surrounded by Neo-Dionysian initiate-revelers. The way they *looked* at her—like she was simultaneously something they wanted to worship, comfort, and consume—made her profoundly uncomfortable. The early years of her transition had taught her not to trust such intent gazes. Attention—whether from transphobes or even other trans people—was never without danger. At any moment it could boil over into hatred and harassment.

Hattie paced around the outskirts of the room, mic in hand, working the crowd, wearing something that was more vineyard than dress. Her original self—in college, long before upload—had been obsessed with trans theology. The idea that trans people were conduits of divine revelation, that they were the yeast from which god made bread, was so appealing in those early years, when the weight of the world's derision stole her ability to love herself.

But that phase of her life had ended when her parents got a call from the insurance company and discovered she was trans. They cut her loose, and in the resulting maelstrom of dysphoria and debt, shame and bad decisions, she hadn't had the energy for metaphysics.

To see that old obsession made manifest was deeply uncomfortable. She understood the desire to make a clean break from the baggage of old religions, but why drape this new creation in the aesthetics of a mystery-cult from antiquity? Why institutionalize it in this way? If Wayland was in charge, she'd have kept the religion and the aid separate. Better to focus on feeding people without tying it to theology.

Above her, on the ceiling, the simulated star-field winked and shimmered. From the room next door, muted by the walls, Wayland could hear the raucous noise of the main dining hall. Even if she was uncomfortable with the novo-religious trappings, she admired what Hattie had built. Free food, clothes, medical-care, and other necessities, supported by the parties and the rituals and a cadre of multi volunteer organizers.

When Wayland was just one person, the organizing she'd been involved with had always been plagued by the problem of volunteers. It was relatively easy to find people who'd come work an hour or two, doing only the sort of tasks they could be trained for in that time. If she was lucky, that type of volunteer might show up again, regularly. Most didn't. And the deep work? The sort that required skill and patience and time and showing up regularly? Who was going to do that? Who was going to connect the man who'd lost disability to other resources? Who was going to manage the irregular supply chain of donated food? Who was going to follow up with all the complex tasks that fell through the cracks? There were never enough people, never enough money to pay them.

Multi-instantiation and the rigor-opportunities of orbital life had ameliorated this problem, and Hattie had built something with more than a decade of longevity and enough power to feed and shelter and heal thousands across dozens of stations.

Hattie's voice fell silent, and Wayland's attention returned to the rite. One of the initiates approached her and put a plastic wineskin to her lips. The wine was sweet and rich with an underlay of the grime-dirt smell of Lenaius Station. She felt parched, so parched, like a withered vine languishing in the dry-cracked dirt. Would the life-giving moisture make her bloom into something new, or wash her away in a landslide of loose dirt?

After the wine, the initiate fed her a thin wafer that she recognized as an edible RFID. As it dissolved upon her tongue, a message flashed in her vision, and whispered in her ears: <I love your cheese; you give me hope I can make my mark on the world like you did.> It was from a Helenite, one of the other Millions lineages.

Another initiate approached, another sip of wine, another message encoded in a wafer. One by one, each of the initiates came to her. Over and over, so many messages of love and appreciation. Sometimes the initiates themselves whispered to her. They shared words of encouragement, spoke to her of the cycle of life, the connectedness of the flesh, of dismemberment and death. They filled her up as if she were a cistern, an endless hole that could never be sated. Her belly stretched and ripened, resting heavy on her lap. When she was younger, she had wanted so badly to get pregnant, to create life within her, to be a mother, to nurture like she had never been nurtured. She had suppressed that dream as best she could—it could never happen, the desire could only hurt her. And now, Hattie had the technology and the resources to do just that. Why did it hurt so much to learn her pain-studded dream was achievable?

Wayland moved her hands around the curve of her belly, feeling the gentle give of the not-flesh, hearing the slosh of liquid inside. What was she made of? It wasn't meat; it felt rough-soft, slightly moist and giving, like sponge-cake, like moss-clad dirt.

Wayland's head was swimming, doing lazy laps in the waters of her memories, each remembrance punctuated by another wineskin, another wafer-message, another adoring adherent. Then she noticed something in her periphery.

The blinking unread message counter. It had haunted her since she arrived at Lenaius. She'd borne that remembrance like a penance, afraid to face the messages or delete them. And now, as she ate another wafer, the message count decreased by one.

These were her unread messages? These well-wishes? These desires for connection? There was no way. Surely these were just the most recent; soon they would reach what she assumed the majority of the messages contained: hatred, pure, unrelenting, and deserved.

She flailed, tried to stand up, but her body was so heavy with wine, like a massive sponge. She wasn't ready to face it. She just needed more time; she needed to escape. An initiate put a wineskin to her lips and told her she was loved, free, blameless.

Her mind lurched, dizzy and off-balance. She felt like she was falling down down down through a roaring void. And then with a sudden impact that took her breath away, she was back in the terror-rage of Crestfall.

She choked on the smoky air, sputtering wine. Millions Nima watched her from the other side of an airlock window. "You made us," she said, her voice traveling impossibly through the growing empty space between them as her module fell to Earth. "You formed us from clay and made us into lambs to be slaughtered." Nima's eight copy-siblings joined her, voices chorusing in rage. "You *murdered* us on a burning pyre. And it was all for nothing."

She was on the floor of her workshop. The basin lay toppled before her, milk flowing around her, scalding her skin. She looked up into the faces that surrounded her.

A woman pointed at her. "You murdered my brother at Crestfall. You botched the module decoupling, you ripped the station's skin open and he fell out into the void." Wayland tasted salt, the tears of her grief, the blood of everyone who died. A child grabbed her hand, their tiny fingernails cutting into her flesh. "I died because of you. I suffocated in my bed, holding my stuffed bear in terror. All my love and all my futures, snuffed out because of you."

"I'm sorry," Wayland whispered. "I'm so sorry, please, please listen." But the crowd didn't listen. A million translucent ghosts accused her. Their voices merged together into a jet-engine roar. From their mouths, they pulled long knives. Wayland closed her eyes. She was going to die; she deserved to die.

And then there was Hattie, beside her. Holding her hand, stroking her cheek. "It's okay. It's okay. You're here, with us, we love you."

Wayland wailed, wine pouring from her tearducts. "I don't deserve it. I shouldn't have copied myself. They're right: I don't deserve to live. I'm a monster. I hate myself."

Hattie pushed something soft and cool and mint-flavored into Wayland's mouth. She swallowed and Hattie held her, the green translucent tulle of her dress wet with the wine-sweat seeping from Wayland's body.

"Wayland, beloved self. The past..." she whispered into Wayland's ear. "...you think it's etched into the universe forever. But it's not real, it doesn't exist, not anymore. What's real is this moment, here. You aren't hurting anyone right now. Let us love you."

"But..." It was hard to think. The room was blinding-bright, the vine-clad walls writhed around her. "The consequences of what I did are real." How many were dead because of her? How many might die because—as Miller claimed—she'd brought the attention of Earth and all its revanchist urges upon the fragile necklace of stations floating in the merciful black?

"You don't need to apologize for trying to protect us. I have nothing to forgive you for. Focus on your body. What do you feel?"

Wayland looked down. "I'm...big." Her body had swelled with the wine. Had she doubled in size, tripled? Hattie clung to the mountain slopes of her waist, the adherents craned their necks to meet her gaze.

"Bigger than you realize," Hattie reached up to stroke Wayland's forearm. "Remember how we used to hunch down, to make ourselves small, to pass unnoticed? The world down there wants to constrain us, conceal us, eliminate us. But we're Millions. We grow, we change, we survive." Hattie's words were slightly slurred, but her eyes were bright, her grip sure. "You don't deserve to be locked up in a tiny workshop, away from everyone else. You deserve the universe, baby, and the universe is really fucking big."

"Deserve?" Wayland wondered. "Does anybody deserve anything? I just don't want to hurt anyone else." She moved her arm to wipe the wine-tears from her face, and felt the world blur and swim around her. Too fast,

her hand smacked herself in the forehead, and fell back.
Hattie screamed in delight as she clung to her. Wayland
wasn't used to being this big yet, her proprioception
hadn't caught up. She wiggled her toes and laughed, her
body an earthquake of flesh, and Hattie laughed with her,
rolling on the unsteady ground of Wayland's engorged
body.

"What do you think?" Hattie asked the crowd. "Is she
done yet?" The initiates cheered, and pulled out forks and
long sharp knives. "Time to feast!"

The crowd fell upon her. They sliced generous cuts
from her thigh, cut her, flensed her. The fed each other
her wine-soaked flesh, stuffing her into each-other's
mouths like couples on their wedding day. She felt herself
becoming smaller, losing herself bit by bit, but there was
no pain, no horror.

Hattie held her hand through it all. "We eat you,
and you become a part of us, your flesh nestled in our
own flesh. We can protect you there, love you there.
Remember, after tonight, you are a part of me. You are
a part of us. And I will fight for you, fight for your cheese
and your cave, and your right to live and grow and
survive."

Hattie kissed her on the mouth, her tongue forcing its
way in, her teeth biting gently at her lips, then fiercely
tearing them away, swallowing them down. She kissed her
cheek, then gnawed it away, swallowed her nose whole.
Wayland lay immobile, a skeleton being picked clean. She
had no more tears to shed, no face with which to smile
her peace and joy. Hattie nibbled gently on her ear and
Wayland shuddered. She still wasn't fine, but if Hattie was
willing to do all this for her, then maybe Wayland could
trust her. Maybe, with time, she could feel worthy of help.

IN THE AFTERMATH of the Neo-Dio initiation, Wayland awoke within the hard metal of her rental body, resting upon the soft mattress of Hattie's bed. She lay there, feeling the formerly fast-flutter of her mind stretch languidly within the repose of beneficial exhaustion. An epoch had passed since she last felt able to float within the waters of consciousness without needing to muddy them with the ripples of thought. She had expected the rites to be hogwash—she had thought she could pass through them and remained untouched—but like water, they had stripped the dirt from her, and only now did she understand how filthy she had been.

Five thousand messages still winked in her vision, and she felt nothing. The dread and guilt would surely return in time, but in the rite's wake she believed she had the courage to delete them. Could she really achieve absolution through inbox zero? The confirmation dialog floated in her vision, tempting her.

And yet, despite the lightness that suffused her now, she couldn't do it. She needed this talisman of guilt to weigh her down and keep her from allowing the impulsiveness inherent to the Millions destroy more lives. But maybe Hattie was right, and she needed to let go of the past and focus on the future she could cook from the ingredients of the present. After all, the countdown timer still ticked ever downward, heralding the imminent heat-death of her cheese cave.

The fates were cruel for forcing her to grapple with her guilt while fighting for her cheese. Wasn't one crisis enough? Two was enough to render her helpless with stress. Three might destroy her entirely. That was a good enough reason to defer dealing with her past.

She closed the deletion confirmation, marked all the messages as *already read*, and removed the unread messages bar from her vision entirely. It was a middle path, and it would have to do for now.

When Wayland emerged from her room, Hattie was ready with a plan. They met in the backroom of the temple-diner, reclining on voluminous artsilk pillows beneath a shimmer-fresco of a satyr with top-surgery scars shooting a medley of foodstuffs from a thyrsus he wielded like a gun.

"You're getting ahead of yourself, Wayland," Hattie said, in between bites of chocolate strawberry. Her mouth and chin were stained red and brown, matching the shimmer-tattoos of bloody swords that danced across her soft brown skin. "If I was Miller, I'd be paranoid about protecting my investment. Keeping all the cheese in one place—like you did—would be a recipe for disaster. If I know the guy—and I do, because I *am* the guy, and more importantly I've been competing against that fuckweasel for decades—he's going to have the cheese in, like, five different vaults, constantly moving."

"So, what, we need to hit all of them at the same time?" Coordinating that sort of intricate operation would be bad enough on Earth, but in space the distance between asteroid vaults might be large enough to involve the messiest bitch in the universe: relativity. Between lightspeed comms delays and orbital mechanics, it was entirely too much for a woman used to working with things the size of a wheel of cheese.

Hattie waved her hand, dismissing the idea. "Nah, hitting the asteroids directly is plan B. Better if we can trick whatever system Miller is using to coordinate all this to bring us the cheese. But again, you're getting ahead of yourself." Hattie took a long swig of thick-black wine, holding up a finger when Wayland tried to say something. "Ahh, fuck this is good stuff. Whatever my other self did to these grapes to make them do that..." She put her fingers to her mouth, made a little chef's kiss. "Come on, get in, you need to try this."

Wayland shook her head. "Hattie, can we stay on topic? The last three times I joined you in there, what was supposed to be a planning meeting turned into another self-fuck."

Hattie frowned sourly. "Your loss. Don't you remember we always get our best ideas post-orgasm?"

Discipline was easier in this body. Wayland stared at Hattie, silent and wanting to be impassive, waiting for her to get back to the point. Hattie stared back, and Wayland was so close to giving in when the other woman finally spoke.

"Fine, whatever, it's not as if I can't find a Millions who actually enjoys being alive." Hattie wiped her mouth, show-daintily. "Ok, so let's say we pull off the heist, we get the cheese. Yay! Except, Miller is gonna notice the cheese is gone. He's gonna know we took it. And he's going to have a very easy time getting Lenaius Station and Earth to work together to make us give the cheese back."

"Because apparently there are now fucking guns in space, according to Miller." It made Wayland want to scream, to hide, to throw a punch. But what would any of that actually achieve? Neither her tears nor her fists could destroy spacecraft. Every Millions remembered living on Earth, a single person powerless against the vast and cruel machineries of the state. That feeling—shed halfway upon becoming multitudinous on orbit—now threatened to overwhelm her again.

"I've...heard rumors, yes." Hattie looked like she wanted to say more. What did she know? None of this was on the newsfeeds. "All the more reason for subterfuge. We need Miller to think he still has his cheese. Do you think you can make counterfeit cheese to fool Miller?"

Wayland laughed. "You're asking me if I can make cheese? Really? But seriously, if you want some shitty mozzarella, I can cook that up in your bathroom sink. You want something close to Red Orion? No. Wait, let me think..."

Wayland stood and began to pace, circling Hattie, thinking out loud. "Getting the cheese looking right on the outside should be doable. RedOrion we can do with a quick brine-bath and some natural food coloring. Herbed Death, we can add the dill and thyme, then dry it in a desiccation chamber.

CometQuake just needs ash from the recycler guild. It's the insides that are going to be tricky..."

"Mmmm, you're so good at this," Hattie murmured. She was staring at Wayland, her chin resting on her hands, her eyes wide, mouth open, her expression a painting of the word *admiration* hung within the museum gallery of her body. Wayland stopped pacing. Pause—two hundred millisecond dissociation—resume pacing.

"Taste and texture are going to be tricky. We don't have six weeks to let the penicillium camemberti and other microorganisms in the cheese develop that perfect solid-ripeness of the rind and creamy-funkiness of the interior. It took me several months to get the workshop Miller bought me spun up and producing significant quantities. And it's not like you have a workshop lying around, or—"

"Bitch, are you dense?" Hattie interrupted. "I literally run a chain of restaurants. I can get you a fully-stocked commercial kitchen. Can you make me some decently convincing counterfeit cheese?"

"Yea, I can make the cheese." There was absolutely nothing that Wayland wanted more. With this body, and a new workshop, she could make magic.

MILLIONS WAYLAND WAS testing her counterfeit cheese when the Waverian ambushed her. Her ear was up against a wheel, her finger tap tap tapping. Did it sound right? Would it fool Miller? He wasn't the most perceptive of the Millions, but he'd eaten enough of her cheese that even he might notice all but the most deceiving of counterfeits.

Tap tap tap. Something wasn't right. It felt so good to be making cheese again, to submerge herself in the work, that glorious admixture of rote technique, intricate experimentation, and strategic iteration. Tap tap tap.

Too dense? She didn't notice the Waverian slithering into the room. Didn't notice the tip-tap tip-tap of ten-thousand mechano-tentacular legs undulating in graceful movement over the rubber-mat floors. Didn't notice until the enormous segmented-metal body of an electro-millipede wrapped itself around her legs and wound its way up her torso.

She screamed, toppled, and the millipede toppled with her. She was on the floor, staring at the ceiling, staring into the eight eyes of the electro-millipede. Wheels of cheese and tools clattered around them.

"Hello, I am glad to meet you," the millipede said when the noise of Wayland's scream died down. "My name is Millions Waverian 55-Hay." Their voice sounded like molten bismuth, and with the digital precision of Wayland's body, she could feel each individual foot caress-gripping her. "You are Millions Wayland, known to the registry as Cheesemaker and Mother of Massacre."

Wayland stiffened, bracing herself for what came next. Millions Wav had been one of the original three copies. Her lineage was obsessed with pushing hard against the limits of dysphoria by inhabiting bodies totally unlike the default human shape. It was incredibly rare to see one; they mostly lived in hard vacuum, doing who-knows-what out at the edges of the station archipelago.

Twenty years ago, the Waverian Consensus had denounced Wayland's efforts to organize protests against austerity and anti-copying laws. They'd publicly and harshly criticized her actions before, during, and after Crestfall. And now that she'd emerged from her workshop, they'd found her at last, and were here to finish the job. She waited for words like knives—or for actual knives—to cut her open.

Instead, Hattie's voice rang out, angry. "What the fuck, 55-Hay. Get off her, give her some space. You know she isn't used to Waverian novo-forms, or their poor etiquette." In her peripheral vision, Wayland could see Hattie's big black boots.

55-Hay didn't move. Despite the strength of her plastiform body, Wayland was trapped beneath the bulk of the millipede. "Millions Hattie, we are here as a favor to you. Did you not ask us to inspect this Wayland-copy? The Waverian Consensus agrees she may be dangerous." The millipede tightened its grip on Wayland as its snake-tongue probe rooted around in her mouth.

Hattie laughed nervously. "Dangerous? That's not what I said. The only thing this one cares about is cheese. If Miller hadn't decided to go full fuckweasel, she'd still be isolated in her workshop. Also, I thought you told us not to mention the whole you-know-what incident? Especially around someone who was involved. Didn't you tell us to move on?"

55-Hay tightened their grip again. Wayland's right knee started sending mechanical failure warnings. She really didn't want to have to adjust to another new body. If she popped out into emulation space, the Waverian would have no reason to crush her. Then they could talk without her being under duress.

But when she pulled up the station's emulation server interface and initiated the transfer request, she got back an indecipherable error code. The fuck? The server was there, signal strength was strong, but transfer kept timing out. She was trapped in her body, trapped beneath the weight of an electro-millipede that she suspected was jamming her attempts to escape.

"The Waverian Consensus believes this one may threaten our long-term project. She has become involved in a delicate situation, and has previously shown poor judgment. I have been sent to evaluate." Tighter and tighter. Wayland tried to move, but the millipede's grip was strong as a vise. Emulated fear looped over and over through her mind, building power with each iteration. "Answer me, Millions Wayland: where do you see yourself in ten thousand years?"

"Uh, what?" Wayland had no lungs to constrict, just a tinny speaker perched behind her pseudo-sinuses. The pressure on her body loosened slightly. She should've expected the Waverian to ask a nonsense question. The Millions had always been weird, but the Waverians in their isolation purposefully chose to crank that up a notch. "Making cheese? Or something like it?" Ten thousand years was such an absurd time frame. Longer than recorded human history. But ten thousand years ago, humans cooked and savored food not entirely alien to modern humans. They even had rudimentary alcohol fermentation, which wasn't far off from cheesemaking in its mechanics. "Look, I can say for certain that in a hundred years, I will not be tired of making cheese. There are *so* many things I'd love to experiment with: new lines to create, new mold strains to test, new ways to use microgravity. If only I had time. I've been crushed with work, trying to meet demand for Miller. And with no help. It's been a lot." After Crestfall, she hadn't wanted to copy herself. What if her copies went off the rails like the Nine Martyrs had? "You Waverians like to take the long view, but ten thousand years is just too much. You can have that future. My priority is the work I need to do right now."

55-Hay went slack and slithered off. "Acceptable. We will Remember these words, and hold you to them."

Wayland didn't like the way they said *Remember*, like they were going to etch her off-the-cuff words onto a tungsten plaque, to last until the universe withered and died. "You messed up my knee." It still flared a failure error; it would probably need to be replaced.

The millipede rippled its body, but didn't have a chance to say anything before the catboy strode in with the strut of someone who knew his legs were long and dangerous. He wore a leather jacket with a wild array of badly-sewn-on patches, and a short black skirt that hid most of his tail.

Two cat ears twitched atop his head, their silver-grey fur matching the multitude of knives strapped and gleaming on his body. Long thin stilettos, short little fish-gutting knives, a Chinese-style cleaver, and a multitude of handleless throwing knives.

Wayland tried to stand up, teetered and failed. Her knee was beyond use. She'd already been physically threatened enough for the day, she didn't need to be filleted by a fucking catboy.

"Heyyy," the catboy purred. He offered his hand to Wayland.

"This is not a Millions," 55-Hay said, declaring the obvious. The Millions were into all sorts of stuff, but the catboy/catgirl aesthetic had never appealed, despite its popularity in certain trans circles decades ago back on Earth.

"Nah, I'm not in your club. Are there really a million of you? Seems implausible." The catboy stuck out his little pink tongue.

Hattie stepped forward. "This is Rascal. He's here to help us infiltrate Miller's restaurant."

Rascal shrugged when Wayland didn't accept his hand, then grabbed a tomato from the counter, pulled out a paring knife, and cut several translucent-thin slices off. He stuffed them into his mouth and savored noisily.

"Are you serious?" Wayland asked. "Where'd you dig up this fossil? There's absolutely no way that Miller is going to hire grandpa catboy here. No offense Rascal, I'm sure you're very talented, but our target likes to appeal to a certain stuffy Earth-based clientele."

Rascal rolled his eyes, grabbed one of Wayland's test cheese wheels and bit into it like it was an apple. His nose wrinkled, he sneezed. "Not as good as your usual stuff."

Hattie grabbed the wheel back from Rascal. "Don't worry, I have a very milquetoast-looking human-form body I'm going to lend him. Rascal has decades of experience working in commercial kitchens, and some of the best knife-skills of anyone I know. Most importantly, he's not a Millions." All of the Millions had experience as chefs, but Miller would be extremely wary of hiring any of them. "55-Hay here is going to ride in Rascal's body and work on the infiltration while Rascal handles the kitchen work. Wayland, your job is to train Rascal and 55-Hay on the layout of Miller's restaurant, and what he looks for in candidates. He's hiring for a single position right now, so we've got one shot to ace the interview." Rascal would need to do a stage—a day-long working interview.

"But I need to keep working on the cheese..." Wayland tried not to whine. She'd finally been able to go back to her work, and now Hattie wanted her to babysit a millipede and a catboy.

Hattie shrugged. "Just copy yourself if you don't have time. You don't need a body to train them, so it should be no problem."

"Yea, no...I'll just handle it myself." Wayland looked at the floor, at the water bath. Anywhere but Hattie's deep brown eyes. Every time she copied herself, things spiraled out of control. There were already enough problems with two Waylands, adding a third was inviting catastrophe. She would just have to work harder, for longer hours. It was no problem—her body didn't tire and her mind had become used to days without rest working in her cheese workshop.

MILLIONS WAVERIAN FIFTY-FIVE Bales of Hay on the Threshold of Eternity—known to their friends as 55-Hay—would not let themselves be distracted by the ecstasy of the sunrise. The curve of the Earth—the home they had forsworn more than one billion seconds ago—whirled terror-fast below them as their cuttlefish ship-body reposed in silent orbit. Here, in the penumbra of the Earth, their ship-skin was cool and quiet, tuned to the music of the spheres and the glitter-crackle of human radio bands.

Distant, aboard Lenaius, their millipede body reclined within the voluminous pillow cascade of Hattie's bedroom. 55-Hay had several other bodies in the vicinity, but their attention was focused on these particular two.

"You were correct to worry about Wayland. Consensus is certain she has been tampered with," 55-Hay said as Hattie plated roasted eggplant, tomato, and goat cheese sandwiches for the temple-diner's next free lunch.

"Tampered with how?" Hattie's body might look entirely unworried, but 55-Hay's millipede body could sense the bloom of glucocorticoids within her blood, the way her flesh primed itself to flee unseeable dangers.

55-Hay rippled their body in a gesture that Hattie ought to recognize as equivocation. "So far, we have only observed the symptoms, not the root cause. It is unlikely that her connectome has been adulterated. This is consistent with our belief that no current power has the ability to directly manipulate cognition or memory."

"Well thank Lady D for that at least." The ability to fine-grain edit a connectome—the map of all neural connections in a body—would be an existential crisis. It would allow manipulating memories, changing personality, and worse. The Waverian Consensus had no desire to explore this technology, and every desire to prevent others from gaining it.

"However, we believe someone has intentionally misaligned her atlas registration."

Hattie sprinkled salt over the tomatoes. "Wouldn't we have noticed that earlier? I had a botched atlas registration during one of my copies and fuck, it was not pretty." If the connectome was the map of all the neurons in a brain, the atlas registration was the key. It told the body integration-translation systems which part of the brain was which, where to listen for neural-activations for specific tasks like left-arm motor-control planning. A misaligned atlas registration meant a brain that couldn't properly interface with its body, resulting in nonfunctional agony.

"We have observed her fine/gross motor control. We have spied on the infrared-bloom from electrical-activation in the neural-core of the work-body you gave her. In this data, we see evidence someone is using her atlas registration to selectively downregulate small areas within her brain-emulation. There is...disagreement within the Consensus as to the reason, but I believe Miller used it to make her focus on cheese-work to the exclusion of all other thought-goals."

"Fuck..." Hattie's brow furrowed and 55-Hay spent a glorious three seconds mapping the complex undulations of the forehead-skin. "Fuck. And fuck Miller. Can you reverse it?"

55-Hay's millipede-body stiffened. "Hold. A moment. I am experiencing." The sun crested the horizon. The pseudo-chromatophore skin of their cuttlefish body sung the chaotic chorus of the sun's electromagnetic rays. Below that sensation-suite was the ocean-deep movement of the Earth's magnetosphere, blown like wave-water by the solar wind. "Sunrise," the cuttlefish said in an electromagnetic aria. "Sunrise," the millipede repeated with sound-waves.

"You guys really like the sunrise, huh?" Hattie's smile was gentle—but her voice sounded brittle with fear for Wayland.

"We designed our bodies to find glory in the danger-wonder of space. Our project is one of millennia, and its final form is/will be incomprehensible to our current mind-bodies. Purpose in our work is not enough. We must find joy. We must *make* joy."

"Cheers to that, buddy." Hattie raised her glass of ginger-beer and drained it. Her eyes narrowed. "Can you fix Wayland?"

It was growing more likely that she understood 55-Hay was evading the question. 55-Hay observed the disposition of Hattie's body. The position of muscles, the scent of the multitudinous brew of hormones, the movement of blood within their web-network of capillaries, and all other things only they could see. They relayed the data to Consensus— the loose cooperative-computational linkage between the other myriad Waverians hidden in the vicinity of Earth— and Consensus offered their analysis. The Hattie-copy's care for the Wayland-copy was genuine and borne of a mix of Millions group-loyalty, admiration for skill-competence, and eros/philautia/agape desire. It was unfortunate then that Hattie had developed her persona to be impulsive-rash as a tool to resist coercion by antagonists to her religio-anarchist operations. Due to this rashness, the Consensus advised caution when sharing the full scope of Waverian movement-plans in this operational theater.

"Determining whether we can restore her autonomy will require direct access to the hardware running her connectome-atlas-integration systems."

"Ok, so what's the problem? If you explain the situation to Wayland, I'm sure she'll let you poke around in her head. Poor thing." Hattie got out the waxed myco-paper and started wrapping half the sandwiches for takeaway.

55-Hay paused before speaking. Not because they needed to choose their words—the Consensus had already provided the words that were most likely to achieve the best result from Hattie—but so that Hattie would understand the caution-importance of what they were going to say. "There may be traps laid within the Wayland-copy. Cognition-bombs; unanticipated dangers. We have already detected one such: someone has placed a bug within Wayland's systems. From snooping on the meta-data streamed from her body to the station's servers, we believe someone is listening, watching, aware of everything Wayland is doing."

55-Hay observed horror bloom across Hattie's face, her hormones spike, hands opening and closing in fear and anger.

"Shit. Fuck, oh fuck, what a fucking cockgoblin of a situation. Why didn't you lead with that? Oh shit, I had her initiated in the secret rites. It's gotta be Miller, he's gonna leak everything, I can't—"

"Respectfully," 55-Hay interrupted. "I do not believe the constructed secrets of your religion are the most important concern."

Hattie stood, began pacing. "No, it *does* matter. You've been out in deep space for too long, you've forgotten what it's like living under the damocles sword of transphobia. Whoever's listening will absolutely use the footage of the rites against us. They'll edit it to make us look bad; they'll pervert our private joy into propaganda."

"Yes, but—"

"Not to mention poor Wayland!" Hattie was in full pace-and-rant mode, sandwiches forgotten. "She came to me for help, and now some asshole is going to use her private grief against her? Absolutely not. She's been through enough; she doesn't need to become a whipping girl *again*. We're going to find out whoever did this and tear them a-fucking-part and then delete that fucking footage."

"Hattie," 55-Hay slithered into Hattie's path, blocking their motion, hopefully blocking the rant as well. "Again, respectfully, there is something more immediately pressing." 55-Hay paused again, focused their eightfold gaze on Hattie's face, so she understood the significance of that brief silence. "You spoke of your heist plan in detail to Wayland. Those details are now in the hands of a potential adversary. You also spoke of the heist to a large crowd of diners when this situation first unfolded. I would gently suggest that you review the opsec guidelines document I will be sending you." 55-Hay did not believe Hattie would actually read the document, but Consensus demanded it be sent anyway.

"Shit shit shit. I hadn't thought of that." Hattie took a moment to compose herself. "See, this is why I like keeping you Wavs around."

"*You* do not keep us, Hattie." The Waverians were not yet untethered from the Earth-umbilical. Many organic volatiles, and complex tool-makers could only be procured from the home that mistrusted them. Hattie was a lifeline to the Waverians. They needed her, but more importantly, they loved her, even if it was often beneficial to constrain her ego.

"Okay, sure." Hattie looked appropriately sheepish. "But—"

"The Waverian Consensus agrees unanimously with the desire to shepherd the autonomy-survival of the human species. We will pave the way, expand the optionality of human futures, and be joyous to exist alongside whatever mutually-beneficial path-choice humanity makes." A partial truth. The inner-system Waverians certainly felt that way, but the blessed multitudes out beyond the asteroid belt were building a future that had grown beyond even 55-Hay's understanding. And the many human-flocks of Earth might never comprehend the strange and beautiful cheeses the Waverians might craft from their milk.

Hattie didn't need to know any of that. Flattery was a more appropriate approach than the fearful and wondrous truth. "You are an important component of our plan to assist Wayland. As such we will be giving you a warning and a gift. Avoid using Lenaius station's emulation servers. Keep your mind running locally. If you need emulation, you may connect to my ship-body. The Waverian Consensus has negotiated a temporary computational-interfacing treaty with the Lenaius station council."

"Ominous." Hattie sat, picked up her shimmer-tattoo kit and raised an eyebrow. "And the gift?"

"The gift is dangerous. We will provide instructions for its use, but will not permit extraneous usage, no matter how tempting." 55-Hay did not agree with the Consensus.

The tool they had made was Bad. Their body understood Hattie and Wayland in a way that could not be translated into raw data for the Consensus to consume. Consensus believe-predicted everything would be fine. 55-Hay did not intend to let their distraction-complacency wreck their mutual hope-desires. And if that meant—as was predicted—that 55-Hay was likely to partially die, then they intended to make the most of their sacrifice.

WAYLAND DIDN'T KNOW what was worse, riding in observer mode in a masculine body, or being in Miller's restaurant again. Hattie had been true to her word, the body she provided the catboy felt incredibly generic: short black hair, brown skin, a forgettable face. Too bad Rascal was entirely unsuited to it; when Miller offered his hand, instead of shaking it, Rascal took it gently in his own hand, brought it to his face and gently nuzzled it.

The look on Miller's face was almost worth the horror she felt as Rascal botched his first impression. It only got worse from there. Hattie had completely oversold his knife skills. Rascal might've been fine working as a line cook in one of those open-plan dining-experience joints, where his fancy tricks and dramatic flourishes would be appreciated, but he absolutely butchered the poor shallot Miller asked him to mince. Wayland took over, moved his hands in the precise rocking motions, leaving a little uncut at the bottom to retain structural integrity while she did the crosscuts.

"Meow," Rascal fucking meowed in annoyance at Wayland.

"Excuse me?" Miller took a step back from Rascal.

"MEOW," Rascal said, louder, as if the problem had been that Miller hadn't heard him. Wayland had to suppress a laugh. This wasn't funny, he was going to flunk the interview.

"Sorry," she said, clearing Rascal's throat. "The, uh, shallots were making me cry, had some gunk in my throat."

"Oh. That's...fine. Why don't I go check on the lobster stock while you, uh, finish up here." Miller obviously thought he was interviewing a lunatic.

<Are you trying to end this interview early?> Wayland messaged Rascal.

<Sorry lol. Old habits die hard,> Rascal messaged back as he flipped his knife in the air and caught it.

What followed was hours and hours of torture. Rascal needed more help than she realized, needed Wayland to be there in his body, moving his hands, teaching him basics that he really ought to know already. She had to be tuned into his body for this, feeling everything he felt: feeling the way his hands were too large; smelling his awful scent as he sweated in the hot kitchen; feeling the rough stubble of their cheek when they wiped away the sweat; roiling in the uncomfortable proprioception of too-wide shoulders. And above all that, spending time with Miller, the man who'd betrayed her, whose piercing gaze felt like it was flensing her skin open to prod and rake at her wounded soul. She wanted to scream, but she had to remain composed, for Rascal's sake, for her cheese.

At the end of the day, Wayland was a raw and quivering mess, hiding deep in the recesses of observer mode, hoping Rascal could manage this last little bit. Miller's restaurant wasn't connected to the station's emulation servers; she couldn't escape until Rascal returned to the temple-diner.

Miller summoned them to his office. The last time Wayland had been here, everything had gone wrong. Was it too much to ask for Rascal to hold it together? Even with Wayland's help, his performance had been mediocre at best. Miller's restaurants were prestigious—and well paying—enough that he could afford to only hire the best.

The idea of Rascal being dismissed, and having to do this interview again, in a different body, made her want to cry.

And yet, Miller smiled, clapped Rascal on the back, and said, "You did a great job today. I'm happy to extend an offer immediately. My general manager will be in touch with paperwork."

<Really? It's that easy? Your plating was atrociously sloppy.> Wayland was confused, suspicious.

"Whatever. He can tell I'm just that good," Rascal said out loud instead of messaging Wayland.

Miller mouth pursed, like he'd licked a sour lemon. "Yes, you are very good," he said, stiffly, then stood and walked back down to the restaurant.

55-Hay, who'd been silent in Rascal's body up until now, messaged just Wayland, <At least you get to go back to your workshop now. I have to stay here inside this feline. I will endeavor to manage his behavior. >

Wayland sighed, silently. She couldn't wait to leave this restaurant, and this body.

HATTIE DID NOT enjoy being stressed all the time. The whole point of being a Millions was to spread the load, to take care of each other, together.

But now the need for secrecy meant everything rested on her. She couldn't trust anyone else with the new heist plan she'd had to cobble together, and she didn't dare copy herself now that the Waverians suspected someone tampering with Lenaius's emulation systems. She was stuck in her party-body, unless she asked the Waverians for help with a transfer, but they were busy shuttling resources in from the outer planets for some big near-Earth operation they'd planned. She didn't want to distract them any more than they already were with her heist.

On top of that, there was a fungal blight in her temple-diner vineyards, and she couldn't figure out how it was spreading, or why it wasn't responding to the usual treatments. Plus all the other normal stresses of running a multi-station mutual-aid and restaurant-cum-nightclub empire.

At least they'd managed to get Rascal into Miller's restaurant. It was a bleak victory. Given that Miller likely *knew* Rascal was a mole—either from his behavior, or the bug in Wayland's brain—he was effectively useless for executing the actual heist. Worse, Miller would surely be planning some devastating counter-play, and she needed to figure out how to handle it without even knowing what it was. *Then* she needed to get other agents hired at the restaurant, without tipping off either Wayland or Miller. This was becoming a shell game—she might be able to pull this off if she could just get Miller to look under the wrong cup. Fuck, it was all too complicated; she felt a migraine coming on.

With everything spiraling out of control, she needed to consider her priorities. Would it be good enough to fool Miller? Could Wayland keep it together until the heist was finished? Saving her cheese was important, yes, but securing the survival and autonomy of the Millions was the real goal. And if she needed to sacrifice the cheese, or Wayland, or herself? She would do it. This was the one central truth of the Millions: they were fungible, expendable, a resource to be spent to secure each other's survival. Wayland had understood that way back at Crestfall when she'd birthed and then sacrificed nine copies of herself for the greater good. Did she still understand?

Hattie wasn't sure, and she was worried about the cheesemaker's increasingly erratic behavior: pacing the station concourse when she wasn't making cheese, staring into the distance, hoarding wheels in cabinets, demanding up-to-the-minute updates on the heist. Hattie had tried to put her off with distractions and reports of vaguely-promising progress, but it wasn't enough. She couldn't give her any real information, not while some unknown third party was listening. Worse, Wayland wanted to know why Hattie was taking the finished counterfeit cheese as soon as it was done, and wasn't satisfied with the admittedly bogus excuses Hattie came up with.

There was only so long she could keep Wayland at bay, only so long before she could no longer put off using the poisonous device the Waverians had gifted her.

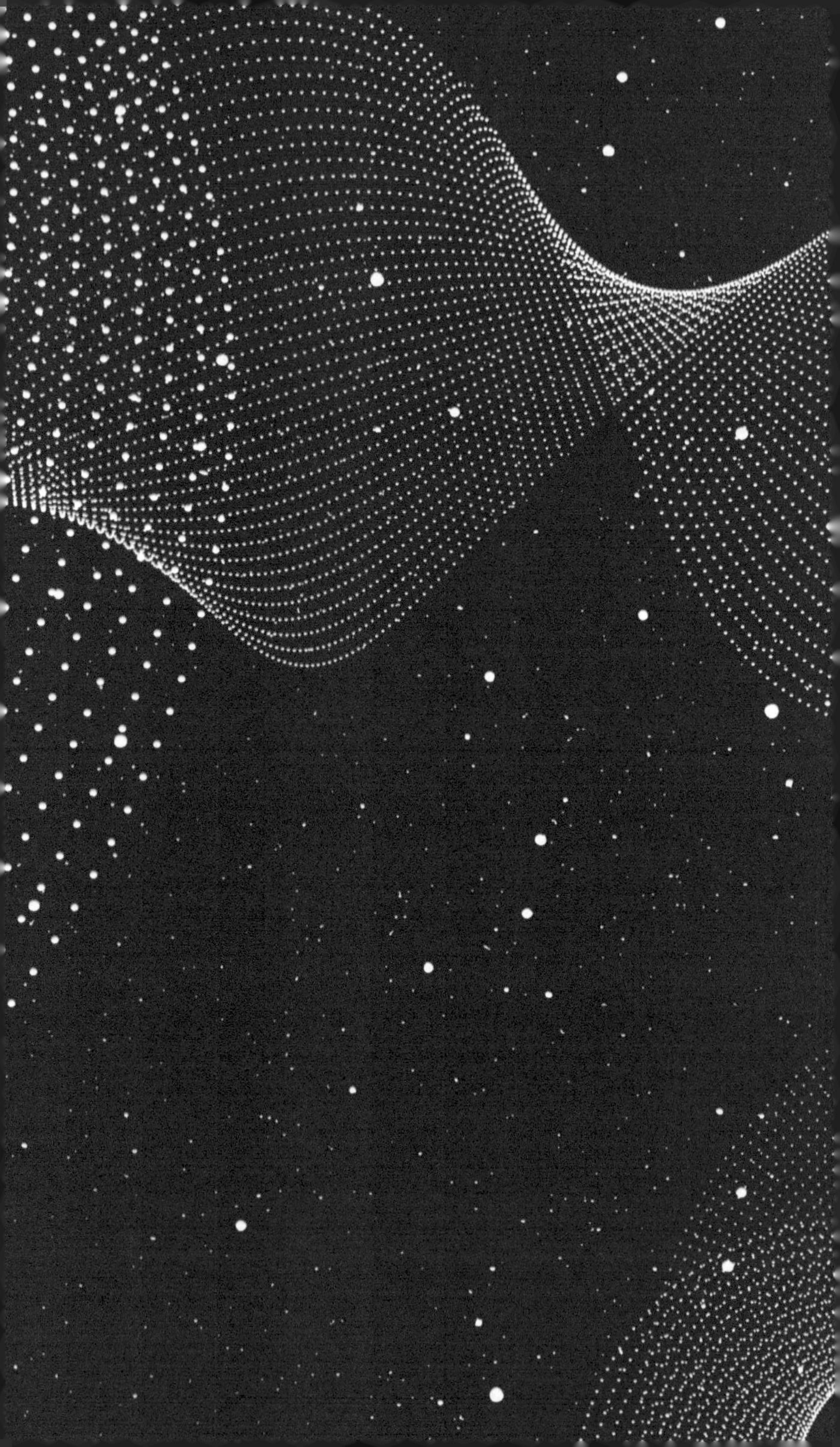

III.

MILLIONS WAYLAND DESCENDED into the bowels of the synth-milk co-op, alone. Less than two hours remained before her cheese cave passed the point of no return. She'd asked Hattie and 55-Hay to spend this moment with her, but they'd blown her off. Apparently they were too busy to comfort her as she watched her life's work burn away.

She found a little nook between two massive bioreactor tanks and settled in, unpacking her lunch: the last small truckle Red Orion she owned, rice crackers, and a tin of station-grown pickled shrimp. The warm hum of the bioreactors was the closest she could get to a hug right now.

She didn't understand why Hattie and the others were giving her the silent treatment. Had she done something wrong? Maybe she was so broken that she inevitably drove away everyone around her. Maybe she'd been right to close herself off from the world. As complicated as cheesemaking was, it was nothing compared to the confusing uncertainties of interacting with other people. A batch of cheese might fail for many reasons, but it would never lie to her, betray her, or abandon her.

As the timer counted down—simultaneously so slow and so fast—she savored the Red Orion. Its variegated mold-white and red-orange rind was supple, like softened leather that gave way easily to the cheese knife. The interior resembled one of those cutaways of Earth's core— the subtle transition from thin rind-surface to cream line mantle to the triple-cream paste core. She'd *made* this. Even though she had failed, even though her cheese cave was doomed, even if the heist seemed like it was going to fail, she could at least be proud of the cheese she'd made. It was enough; it had to be enough.

Wayland ate the last bite of cheese as the timer reached zero. The timer wasn't a perfect estimate, but it wasn't as if something unexpected was going to happen in the next hour or day that would completely change the trajectory of the asteroid—or the heist.

She curled her knees close to her chest and rocked on the floor for a half-hour, before cleaning up her lunch and then ascending from of the bioreactor room. Time to go back to the kitchen and hope that work could distract from the grief of her failure.

She'd walked this route on dozens of occasions, enough that she'd stopped really paying attention. And yet, each time she passed by the luxury boutique, she found herself staring at the display advertising her cheese. Today, the display was bigger, announcing a new shipment of cheese, with a single half-wheel of Red Orion sweating gently on a cheese-stone.

If she'd been in an organic body, she might've been distracted by her mouth watering or her stomach rumbling. But in her plastiform work-body, priming her taste-smell-texture sensory suite was a conscious act. Which left plenty of attention for noticing that the color of the rind was slightly off, barely enough to be noticeable, but glaringly obvious to Wayland with the upgraded visual acuity of her synthetic eyes.

This meant two things. First, she needed to adjust the fake dye she was using to simulate aging to account for long-term degradation. Second, it meant that Hattie had betrayed her. This was clearly a wheel of her counterfeit cheese, and because they hadn't yet managed to find Miller's vault, Hattie must be selling the counterfeit cheese instead of saving it to swap with the real cheese Miller had hidden.

Wayland curled her fists hard enough that they flared mechanical stress warnings. First Miller, now Hattie. Were all her other selves irredeemable untrustworthy bastards?

She swiveled on rubber-soled feet. Tourists parted before her, their faces terrified at the monstrous six-foot-five woman sprinting down the concourse. She burst into the temple-diner, a keening roar on her lips, her arms raised in anger.

"Hattie!" she screamed as the diners felt silent around her. "What have you done with my fucking cheese?"

Hattie descended her throne, a bland smile on her face. "Wayland, baby, you are making a scene." She approached Wayland, grabbed her raised hand, pulled her arm down. "I can explain, but not here," she whispered.

Wayland followed Hattie to her bedroom, fuming. She was done with excuses, done with betrayal. Either Hattie explained herself—and the explanations were acceptable—or Wayland would walk away from it all. Fuck the cheese, fuck her cave, fuck all the other Millions.

She would start anew, alone. She would build her power, become a lineage to herself, and—if she desired—she would work towards revenge. Maybe the best revenge was thriving free from the machinations of the Millions. Maybe Miller's approach had been right all along.

The bedroom door closed behind them. Hattie pulled one of her plush stuffed animals down from a shelf and snuggled it. The stuffed bunny had big floppy ears and glassy eyes. Most of the other animals looked worn with love, but this one was out-of-the-box new.

"I'm so sorry I haven't been more forthcoming," Hattie said, her voice cracking. Wayland couldn't interpret what that emotion was, but it was intense. "Everything is spiraling out of control, and..." She paused, bit her lip, debating something inside her head where Wayland couldn't see.

"No more excuses Hattie. Tell me what's going on, in detail. I want the logs of your messages with 55-Hay and Rascal. I want you to tell me your copy-lineage in the registry isn't a fake. I want you to convince me you aren't selling my counterfeit cheese on the side."

"I can't!" Hattie cried out. Were those tears in her eyes? "Just...do you trust me?"

"No." Wayland said. It was a complete sentence. "But I respect you enough to give you a choice. Either come clean, or I'm walking over to Miller's restaurant and asking 55-Hay and Rascal directly."

Hattie froze. "You're serious." She hugged the stuffed bunny tight, clearly shaken by Wayland's ultimatum. "I guess I don't have much choice do I?" Her voice was soft, her eyes watered.

"No. I've already been betrayed once. If I can't trust you, there's no point."

"Fine. I was just about to meet with 55-Hay anyway. I'd invite you along, but you know how persnickety they are about opsec. Here, you can ride in my body, and if they complain, I'll tell them it was my idea. "

Wayland felt a rush of relief. Her paranoia had been unwarranted; there was nothing to worry about. She'd had so many upheavals in the last few weeks. If Hattie had betrayed her, she wasn't sure she could handle it.

Wayland leapt into Hattie's body.

Hattie's body was warm and soft—so so soft—and so so small. Wayland looked up into Hattie's eyes—such beautiful brown!—and felt her thoughts slow. She wiggled her nose in confusion. Her long ears twitched. Why was she looking up at Hattie? Why was Hattie's smile so sad? Why couldn't she reach up to caress her cheek? Oh. She wasn't in Hattie, she was in the plush bunny.

"I'm so so sorry dear," Hattie said, and hugged Wayland tight. It was the best hug Wayland had ever had in her entire life, there was nothing like being so soft and being hugged by someone so soft. "I know this is wrong. I know this feels like a betrayal but..." Hattie sniffed. "We're doing this for you. I can't let you interfere with my plans. You'll thank me later." Hattie winced. "I hope."

Wayland tried to move, tried to struggle out of Hattie's embrace, but her muscles were weak, made to move a tiny polyester body . She couldn't prevent Hattie from placing her up on the shelf, next to all the other stuffed animals. Hattie gave her a single sad glance, then seemed to move stop-motion quick out of the room. Wayland felt so slow; everything else was moving so fast.

Her thoughts thickened into crystallized honey; it took three tries before she was able to send the command to leave the plush body, but the station didn't respond. She wasn't a person, the error code said. Inanimate objects couldn't be emulated. She whimpered, but no noise came from her polyester flesh. The numbers of her internal clock spun fast, then faster. There wasn't enough computational power in the toy's little processors. She swirled down, losing bits of herself, having to put more and more cognition threads into virtual memory.

How could Hattie do this to her? The one mercy of this
trap was that she couldn't feel the full sting of betrayal.
She clung to what little splinters of rage she had like a raft,
just barely keeping her mind floating up above the vast
depths of dream-like unconsciousness that threatened to
envelop her. If she gave in, if she let the waters swallow her
up, she was convinced she would become nothing more
than an inanimate archive of a human. A lonely memory,
a bunny sitting on a shelf.

HATTIE KNEW THAT sometimes divine providence was
a real bitch. How else could she explain the fate of this
beautiful broken cheesemaking version of herself? To
have lost everything she held dear, to have come to Hattie
for help, only to be betrayed. Surely this was some cruel
punishment of the gods. Because if not? Then this whole
situation was entirely *her* fault, and that...didn't bear
thinking about.

If only Wayland hadn't given her that fucking ultimatum.
If only she'd been more trusting—but who could blame
her after Miller betrayed her? If only Hattie could've told
her the truth. If only Wayland wasn't bugged. If only they
all weren't fighting for survival against a whole fucking
planet that wanted to pave over them with its own need for
conformity. If only...if only...

But no, she was fully committed. No turning back now.

Hattie held the bunny in her lap, stroking its soft
polyester fur. "I wuv you soooo much," the bunny said
with a saccharine voice.

"I love you too," Hattie replied guiltily.

TIME MOVED FAST; time moved slow. Wayland was a bunny; Wayland was a solitary burning rope, a single cognition thread, the flames of her rage the only thing keeping the waters of involution at bay.

Hattie hugged her, stroked her ears. "You are going to make me so much money." Hattie's voice? Miller's? It was all the same. Wayland stared at the ceiling, unable to move her head to look anywhere else. Hattie held her as she slept, each of her snores lasting two seconds, lasting ten thousand years.

"I hate you," Wayland said, but the bunny wasn't programmed to say those words. The closest match the body-integration system could find within the bunny's stock phrases was, "I wuv you soooo much."

Wayland howled and the bunny-body laughed. Hattie snuggled her tighter.

"I wuv you soooo much."

"I wuv you soooo much."

"I wuv you soooo much."

"I wuv you soooo much."

The words were like a prayer, no meaning behind them except the raw rage that kept her alight.

"I—" What? "I—" What did she hate? Who did she love? She was on a shelf, alone again. The room was still, no stimulus to spark the fire, the waters rising, her mind drowning. She was gone.

She awoke to another embrace. An electro-millipede held her in its ten thousand hand-feet. How long had she slept? Had the Waverian's ten-thousand years passed so quickly? Surely all had crumbled to ashes in that time, no more cheese, no more flesh to hunger with. If her other self still lived, she would know she had failed.

"This is going to hurt, a great deal," the millipede said, flatly.

It hurt worse than that. It hurt worse than copying herself, hurt worse than betrayal, worse than losing herself inside a bunny. Her brain was a shallot and the millipede

wielded ten thousand knives. But a shallot was such
a small thing, and her brain was vast. Every time she
thought surely it was over, the blades found another onion
layer to slice, and every cut wept poison-white juice that
burned her sense of self.

"Is it working?" A voice like a thumb in her eye asked.

"No." The word was a gunshot. "This connectome is
permanently damaged. What was done to her was butcher's
work. Unconscionable. I will try once more, for purely
educational purposes, then delete her."

"Poor thing. Make it quick."

Wayland screamed and if the bunny's giggle sounded
maniacal, it was entirely her imagination. When oblivion
came, it was nothing but relief.

MILLIONS WAVERIAN FIFTY-FIVE Bales of Hay on the
Threshold understood with crystalline clarity the full
extent of their miscalculation. If they were Hattie, they
would say this was divine punishment for hubris. The
Waverians had believed themselves to be the masters of
multi-instantiation technology. Yet here lying before them,
in this bunny, in this cheesemaker's mind, was evidence
they had been surpassed. The vast resources of fetor
and fertile Earth had birthed a horror in secret, and the
Waverians were powerless to reverse it.

"I cannot," 55-Hay said to Hattie as she stared at the
flayed bunny. "I cannot excise the rot. I cannot in good
conscience continue this work, knowing I will fail and my
failures are torturous to a hundred Waylands."

The poison pill in Wayland's connector was a crude
and nasty piece of work. While it was simple in its
construction compared to the wild, infinitely complex
overgrowth of a human brain, it was deeply integrated

into her somatosensory cortex, her auditory cortex, and her entire occipital lobe. Everything Wayland saw, heard, or touched, was recorded and unconsciously transmitted to unknown observers. Interestingly, whoever had done this had missed that messages sent on an internal feed were processed in a different location. Those were unlikely to be recorded.

Initially, 55-Hay had hoped they could merely tune Wayland's atlas registration to ignore the connectome region the rot was in. But the rot was cleverly designed. It was diffuse enough that excising it directly caused cascading cognition failures, and downregulating it via the atlas registration rendered Wayland blind, and deaf, lacking any sense of touch and a number of other senses. Recovery—or working around the problem via neuro-prosthetics—was a possibility, but only with years of physical and cognitive therapy. The situation in the restaurant was rapidly devolving; they needed Wayland *now*.

"Fuckshit. Ok, we can handle this. Roll with the punches." Hattie's eyes flashed and 55-Hay knew she was about to do something foolish. "New plan. Miller's been three steps ahead of us this whole time. The only way we can disrupt his plan is to make things as chaotic as possible."

She grabbed the bunny and ran towards the door.

"But—" 55-Hay objected, moving to block her. Chaos was a threat to the Waverians' long-term plans. They stopped halfway, interrupted by a data-dump from their companion-in-orbit, 99-Barrels. "I am sorry, I must deal with an emerging situation in orbit."

Hattie grinned. And then she was gone, through the door, taking what remained of Millions Wayland.

WAYLAND AWOKE IN an unfamiliar body, surrounded by the comforting clamor of a restaurant kitchen. Here was a cutting board, a chef's knife in her hand, a bundle of fresh parsley to mince. She rested in observer mode, letting the back and forth of the knife's rocking motion comfort her. Then she remembered: the bunny, the betrayal.

Her hand trembled, the knife wavered. It wasn't her doing; she was still in observer mode, but whoever's body this was could surely feel the ocean of emotion roiling behind that thin wall of motor-control permissions.

<Wayland, this is Hattie, please stay calm, we're in Miller's restaurant. Be careful.>

Wayland typed out and deleted three different responses before deciding on simply, <Why?> What possible justification could Hattie have for what she'd done?

<I'm so sorry. We had to. Your brain was compromised. Miller fucked with your atlas registration to make you more compliant, to make you focus on the cheese.>

Wayland wanted to take control of the body just so she could laugh. <Are you serious? You think I'd let Miller mess with my head? *I* was the one who edited my atlas registration. I wanted focus. I *needed* it. After Crestfall, it was either that or permanent dissociation.>

<WHAT?> Hattie was slack-jawed, not bothering to chop herbs anymore. <Why didn't you tell us that? Fuck!>

<It's none of your business what I do with my brain. And it doesn't excuse trapping me in a fucking bunny.>

"Laurie, the fuck's wrong with you? If you can lean, you can clean!" One of the other chefs was yelling at them. Hattie shook her head and went back to chopping.

<I'm sorry. I'm sorry. But it wasn't just the atlas registration. Someone put a bug in your connectome, to spy on you. I'm sorry, we couldn't get it out. They're still listening. We don't think they can listen to the internal message feed, but we aren't sure.>

<Oh. Shit.> Wayland flailed inside her head. The sensation of knowing her own cognition was compromised resembled nothing so much as that time in college a bee had flown up her dress and her senseless panic had drowned out any understanding of where the bee was in her clothing. The bee had died—either from her thrashing, or from the sting it gifted her in its fear. <I'm still furious at you. You have no idea what it was like, being trapped in the bunny.>

Whatever response Hattie had was drowned out by the sound of a ladle banging a metal hotel pan.

"Everyone, over here! Team meeting," Miller shouted. The kitchen quieted, the silence reminding Wayland of the way all noise was attenuated during a hull breach, as the sound-transmitting, live-giving air fled into the void.

Miller stood on an upturned hotel pan, holding a woman by the lapel of her stained white chef's uniform. The kitchen crew crowded around them. Wayland didn't recognize the woman, but the confused fear in her eyes felt far too familiar.

<This is it, Wayland. Keep quiet and enjoy the show.>

Miller cleared his throat, obviously relishing the awkward anxious energy of the crowd. "You thought you were so clever. You thought I wouldn't notice my own self riding these bodies?" He gestured at the woman he held. Out of the corner of her eye, Wayland saw the body Rascal was hiding in flinch and then turn to flee. A dishwasher grabbed him and dragged him before Miller. "You thought I wouldn't see the fucking speech Hattie made in front of a huge crowd about how she was going to heist me?" He took the time to glare at the two bodies he suspected of being Millions. "You've failed. You're fired, and you bet I'm going to have the station council and the trans-orbital court burn your asses so hard you won't be able to dock at any station within a hundred AU."

Miller paused as Hattie strode forward. Wayland felt their mouth curl into a wicked grin.

"You poor thing," Hattie said, reaching up to put a hand on his cheek. "You have no idea what's going on, do you?"

He flinched at her touch, tried to step back, and fell off the hotel pan with a yelp as his butt hit the rubber-mat floor.

Hattie leaned over him. "You're right. We never found your little stash. But why would we bother? You've been bringing wheel after wheel of Wayland's best to this restaurant. And we've been exchanging wheel after wheel of Wayland's best for Wayland's worst. Every wheel you've served in the last few weeks was a fake. The real cheese is in *our* possession. Every certificate of fractional ownership you issued to a diner was done fraudulently. And—" She theatrically pushed an ethereal button, "—now the world knows. I told you I would ruin you for what you did to Wayland."

"No..." Miller whispered. "You didn't. Oh fuck."

"I'm going to give you a choice, Miller. Either we leave you to your fate, let your creditors tear you apart. Or..." She paused, glared at him. "Or, you let me buy you out, tell me where the rest of the cheese is, *and* apologize to Wayland. What'll it be? Every moment you delay, your fortune falls further."

Miller panicked, grabbed a wooden spoon and tried to throw it at her, but missed. It clattered uselessly against a distant stock-pot. "I was trying to help you," he screamed. "Do you have any idea what people on Earth think of us? Do you care? Degenerates! Why can't you be normal? Earth is coming. They're already here. You have no idea what I've been protecting you from!"

Hattie kicked him. "Then tell me, asshole."

"What?"

Hattie leaned in close, giving Wayland a closeup of Miller's fear and confusion. "If you actually had a good reason for screwing Wayland over, I want to hear it."

MILLER FELT LIKE a balloon, overinflated for so long, with nothing but two fingers pressed against the latex sphincter to keep the mounting pressure in. And now, in the moment of his abject failure, a simple question—*why did you do it?*—had released those fingers, let all the air that was keeping him afloat sputter out. He was deflated, falling in on himself. Hattie sat next to him, cross legged, waiting, listening. He lay back, resting his head on the dirty rubber mat floor, and spoke.

It began with an officer of the trans-orbital court in Albuquerque serving him papers as he sat down for a meal in his own restaurant. His food lay uneaten as he read the documents. A private equity firm—Deskrope LLC—had bought the company that had originally developed the technology he'd used to upload and copy himself all those decades ago. They claimed their ownership of that defunct startup's intellectual property extended to all the Millions and the derivative tech they'd developed: the emulation servers, the copying algorithms, the systems used for interfacing a connectome to an atlas registration to a body, and—worst of all—the very bodies and minds of the Millions themselves.

The Millions-copies weren't people, the lawyers argued. They were code; they were machines for running that code; they were a process by which those machines and code could be replicated. They were intellectual property, and they belonged to Deskrope LLC.

None of it made any sense. That's not how intellectual property works, he argued with his lawyers. But, the laws had changed since he'd left Earth, they replied. He'd lost that first court case, but at least he'd been smart enough not to travel down to Albuquerque in person. He appealed; he failed. Letters full of increasingly-less-polite legal knives piled up in his inbox. He tried to explain to the lawyers that he had no control over the Millions; he couldn't force them to turn themselves in—nor would he, he hastily added, when Hattie glared at him.

Deskrope wasn't going to let their investment go to waste. They talked to a different sort of lawyer; they talked to senators; they talked to others who needed a way to enforce Earth law—American law—in space. Miller wasn't there, he didn't know how they did it, but when the US Space Force came for him he knew he was fucked.

So he settled. Deskrope was willing to back off, to license the tech on a temporary basis, in exchange for regular exorbitant payments. But Miller didn't have the money. His restaurants were doing well, but the settlement specified a number an order of magnitude more than the liquid assets he had available.

Hence the cheese. He admitted to Hattie that the plan seemed harebrained, but it had worked! At least for a while. Until Hattie messed everything up.

Miller didn't mention his side deal. He didn't want to know what Hattie would do to him if she found out he'd promised Wayland to Deskrope.

None of the other Millions understood how lucrative Wayland's cognition tweaking could be. That line of research had been heavily restricted by the One Person One Instance Treaty, and after Crestfall, the major biotech corporations had scuppered their plans for extrajudicial orbital labs. Now that investor confidence was returning to orbit, firms like Deskrope were willing to do just about anything to exploit the tech the multis had built. Such intense corporate desperation was like a tidal wave that threatened to wash away everything he'd built. Selling out one of his copies seemed like a fair price to pay to secure his own future, and the future of the rest of the Millions.

"Hey, asshole," Hattie shoved his shoulder. "Why didn't you ask for help?"

Miller felt laughter rising, uncontrolled, frantic, maniacal. "Are you serious? Do you really think Deskrope would have negotiated with *you*? This problem needed someone serious working on it, someone the court would respect, someone the court thinks is a real person."

Hattie rolled her eyes. "We could've helped you raise money, so you wouldn't need to screw over Wayland."

Miller rolled his eyes. "As if you would've ever helped *me*. Admit it; you'd have used the situation to fuck me over."

"I..." Hattie looked at her hands, her voice soft. "We can still help, still salvage something from this disaster."

"Help? Pffft, whatever. You want to buy me out? Fine. I'll give you everything. This is officially your problem now. I am taking a vacation." The Millions were always criticizing him, excluding him, kicking him while he was down. Now it was time for them to learn it wasn't easy being Miller; time for them to learn everything he did for them.

"Okay." Hattie patted his shoulder. "We can work out the details later. Where's the rest of the cheese?"

Miller opened his mouth. He was so close to telling the truth when inspiration hit like a bolt of wicked lightning. There *was* a way out of this situation, a way to clear the board, to remove his greatest rival, and get everything he wanted.

Miller laughed, tried to stop, failed, held up his finger, and then finally said, "I can't believe you never found it. It's been here on Lenaius the whole time, right under your feet. Lower spire warehouse unit W113-S. Good luck with it! It's brought me nothing but trouble; I hope it brings you the same."

Hattie's face shifted subtly: her expression softened, her shoulders drooped slightly. "This is Wayland." Her smile was sad. "I will always appreciate what you did for me. Giving me the workshop, letting me save myself through my work. Sometimes..." She paused, winced, her eyes watered. "I worry we Millions aren't really fit to be people, that we're destined to hurt everyone around us.

And yet we just keep making more of ourselves, more pain to spread around. I...I'm sorry it ended like this. You should've trusted me."

Miller looked away. Why should he feel guilty? After all, there were always more Millions. The real cheesemaker was still safe, back in the workshop. And if his plan worked, there would be no-one left to remember his sins.

He looked up and smiled sadly. "Just remember, everything I did, I did to protect you."

No-one spoke in the service elevator on the way to Miller's vault. The silence wrapped Hattie like a wet blanket, dousing the hopes she'd had that confronting Miller, and getting the cheese back, would fix things between her and Wayland.

Wayland stood, immobile and inflexible as a caryatid, eyes fixed on the elevator's slowly ticking floor-number display. The tension in the air lay thick and noxious as a slice of limburger. 55-Hay in their electro-millipede, and Rascal in his cat-eared body, stood next to her, exchanging wary glances.

<Talk to me?> Hattie messaged Wayland. She hated not being able to speak with the whole of her body, conveying meaning not just with text but the chorus of muscle and skin, eye contact and positioning. <I'm sorry. Please just talk to me?>

Silence. Hattie hated the idea that after Wayland got her cheese back, she might lock herself up in her workshop for another two decades or more. She deserved better. They were so close to the end; Hattie had one last chance to make things right. But what could she even say?

"Wayland, talk to me," Hattie said, out loud. Rascal flinched at the sudden noise, but Wayland remained impassive. Fuck the bug; let whoever was listening hear. Making things right with Wayland was more important.

Hattie reached out, gripped Wayland's arm and tried to pull her around, but her flesh was no match for Wayland's huge piezo-muscles. "Please. I'm so sorry. But...I hope—seeing the results—it was worth it?"

"Worth it?" Wayland sounded confused. Better than angry, right? "Do you really think *anything* could be worth that?"

"But, the you-know-what, and...well, we had—"

"If the next words out of your mouth are 'we had to,' I swear I will find a way to eject this fucking elevator into space just so I can watch the oxygen boil out of your lungs and your lying fucking mouth. You could have told me, you could have—" Wayland let out a little cry of anguish, then went silent. Rascal glanced at Hattie, mouthed a silent *wow* behind Wayland's back.

Five floors passed. Really, what did Wayland think Hattie could have done differently? And why wasn't 55-Hay defending her? The truth was, Hattie did feel guilty. What she'd done was wrong, but—well, maybe now wasn't the time for excuses.

The elevator stopped; the door opened. They had arrived, but Wayland didn't move. Hattie cringed a little in anticipation, but all Wayland said was, "No. It wasn't worth it. I...appreciate your help, but once I get my cheese back, we're done. I'm going to hire an ombudsperson—not one of yours—and there's going to be consequences for you. No more of those toys, no more traps, you'll have to pay sanctions."

"That's fair." Hattie sighed. "You're right. It wasn't worth it. If I'd known how bad it was going to be, I wouldn't have let the Waverians talk me into it. I'm sorry. I don't expect you to forgive me, but—"

"What?" Wayland whirled, glaring at 55-Hay. "*You* made the bunny? And you let Hattie take the blame for it? Do you have anything to say for yourself?"

55-Hay rippled their foot-pads and tilted their head. "I would hope you would empathize with our decision, having also been driven to extreme measures by an extreme threat."

Wayland flexed her huge rubber hands. "Really? Really? This situation isn't comparable *at all* to Crestfall. You have a lot of explaining to do if you want—"

"Yes, we owe you a great deal of information. But much will be clear to you when you see the situation in Miller's vault. We must hurry." And with that, 55-Hay slithered past Wayland, out the elevator and down the hall.

Wayland followed them, ignoring Hattie trying to pull her back, ignoring Hattie's words. She stifled the urge to scream. What was the point of any of this if she lost Wayland?

WAYLAND PAUSED AT the airlock door to warehouse W113-S. Hattie sniffled behind her, but Wayland ignored her. The woman was desperate for absolution, but for now, Wayland needed space. She needed her cheese, she needed to return to her workshop. If it was too late to re-integrate, maybe her other self would be willing to accept help. Surely she would need it—disentangling herself from Miller and going independent would be a mountain of work.

The outer airlock door accepted the code Miller had given her. They entered the airlock, waited as the outer door closed and locked, as the inner door to the warehouse opened.

"The fuck?" Hattie threw up her arms in confusion. "What is all this?"

"Where's the cheese?" Wayland asked.

"We are going to die," 55-Hay whispered to themselves, unheard in the roar of the cooling fans.

"Mrow?" Rascal scratched his head.

There was no cheese. The warehouse was full of server-racks, their LEDs blinking green, red, yellow. A cold wind blew around them.

"Maybe it's in the back," Wayland said. They walked into the warehouse, peering around servers, looking for the cheese.

Crack! Wayland staggered; her internal feed filled with errors. She looked down at the puckered hole in her plastiform chestplate. A gunshot?

She dove behind a server. *Crack! Crack!* Wayland watched as Rascal threw a knife into the throat of a man wielding a wicked looking gun.

Crack! She stood, ran towards the door. Lightning flashed from 55-Hay's body, arcing randomly to server-rack, railing, floor, gun.

Someone screamed.

Crack! A new hole appeared in her side. More errors cascaded too fast to read. She fell to the ground, plastic smacking against the kevlar-draped aluminum floor. Her left leg was inoperable. She turned her pain off, dampened her panic.

Crack! A man stood before her wearing grey-spattered camo. He leveled his rifle at her head, resting the butt in that perfect groove beneath his collarbone.

Crack; the muffled sound of the bone in his leg breaking as Wayland's arm shot out to grip and twist it. Her body wasn't flesh—she could push the peizo-electric motors of her body past their safe tolerances. She could damage her shell beyond repair, just for a chance to escape. The man fell; she caught him, her arm wrapped around his neck, strangling him unconscious.

Crack! She crawled towards the door. Oh, there was a hole in the floor, a puckered wound in the aluminum, a hull breach. Smoke swirled down through the hole, escaping into the void. Instinct told her to stop: she needed to plug the hole. No, this body didn't have lungs, didn't need air; Wayland needed to escape.

Crack! Another hole, more errors. Her body refused to do more than spasm. She'd been so close. Now she was going to die. Her copy at the workshop would never know what she'd sacrificed, how she'd failed.

"Hey, I'm gonna get you out." Here was Rascal, dragging her, pausing to throw a knife at an approaching soldier. He was stronger than he looked—Wayland's cheesemaking body weighed at least one-hundred and fifty kilograms. "It's going to be okay. If we can just get to the airlock, I can—" He screamed. Wayland was facedown, she couldn't even turn her head to see what struck him.

Silence. No more gunshots, no more screams. The cooling fans had shut off, the air lay still and heavy. Footsteps behind her, four pairs of hands lifting her, dragging her to a room. Here were the others: Hattie and Rascal bound by zip-ties and 55-Hay restrained with metal vises, all surrounded by men with wicked-long guns and vacsuit-armor.

A man wearing a polo-shirt and khakis looked her up and down. It was the same sort of disdainful leer-and-chuckle she remembered from when someone would clock her back on Earth. Which was ridiculous, because her body ought to read *big fuckOff robot* more than *man* or *woman*. "This one's the AI?" he asked.

"Yes, sir," a voice behind her answered.

"Good, prep it for immediate extraction. Remove the cognition core and mem-crystals intact. Then destroy the body. Keep the fat one on ice. Do an EMP on the bug-looking one; full sweep, make sure there's nothing left in there. Bag the remains; out of sight. Fucking thing gives me the creeps."

"Yes, sir. What about the, uh, cat?"

Homme strode over to Rascal, looked him over, made a disgusted face. "Well, fuck me. Why'd you do this to yourself, son?"

Rascal snarled and spit in Homme's face.

"Cat got your tongue?" No one laughed at Homme's joke. "This thing's not on the list. Kill it."

Wayland screamed, wordlessly, tried to struggle out her bindings, but her body only responded to her commands with a log full of errors.

"No!" Hattie yelled. "Kill me instead. He didn't do anything wrong. He's just a...a fucking cat. What kind of a monster kills a cat? I'm the one who planned all this. Kill me."

Homme laughed. "Kill you instead? This isn't some—" he put his hands in the air, looking for words. "Whatever, I don't need to be arguing with you." He got up in Hattie's face. Wayland could just barely hear him whisper. "You're not a person, just a little computer program that thinks it's hot shit. We let you tranny AIs run loose too long, breeding like rats, becoming an existential threat to *real* humans. No more. We're gonna ship you back to Earth and put you in a nice little computer where you can work work work all day and all night, and pay off all the damage you've done up here. Doesn't that sound nice?"

Hattie opened her mouth, but Wayland never heard her surely devastating retort. One moment she was a mind, living and thinking in a plastiform body. The next, she was an inanimate lump of plastic—titanium, neuro-transistor, doped-silicon, and mem-crystal—extracted and held firmly in the hand of a soldier.

MILLIONS HATTIE AWOKE—not knowing she had died—into the wrongness of a body that wasn't hers. The first sensation that came to her was bone-sucking coldness. A shiver in her spine, and hard cold thighs touching a cold metal bench.

"Time to wake up, sister." A voice, warm and feminine. "Your work isn't done. We anticipated you would want to be alive for what happens next."

Proprioception came slowly—a blessing, because she did *not* like what she felt. Her new body was superficially shaped like her old one, short and round and wicked. But it wasn't right. Metal bones and metal skin, held together with piezo-rubber muscles, like a mollusk's dream of the human form. Terribly strong and durable, yes, but not the beloved softness of her hard-won flesh body.

Hattie scream-roared, but the speaker-produced noise lacked the pleasing diaphragm-ruble of organic rage. "No. No. Not again, not again." She repeated the words over and over, the mantra a feeble attempt to blot out the jolt-horror of waking up in a foreign body.

"Yes, again." The voice came from an electro-hydra. A sinuous body with seven heads and six utility-tentacle feet. "Forty-seven minutes ago, your registry beacon confirmed fatal termination. Your copy predecessor is dead—or worse. My condolences." The hydra bowed her heads for exactly ten seconds in some sick Waverian idea of providing space for bereavement. "We restored you from backup. How many fingers am I holding up?" The appendage the Waverian waved in front of her face was complicated enough to give a taxonomist a migraine.

The motion overwhelmed her visual processing. Another wave of dysphoria struck, severing the clean connection between self and body. All her senses felt delayed, like the echo on a bad connection. This body had no lungs; she couldn't do the breathing exercises she usually used to center herself. She fell to the floor, squeezing her hands hard hard hard just to feel some control.

Time passed, on the floor, until she'd regained enough of herself to focus on her environment. Where was she?

If she'd died less than an hour ago, that meant somewhere close. Linen tapestries depicting rampant dinosaurs and flying saucers covered the faux-stone walls. Above her, an oval skylight revealed a glorious pearl-blue sky, like a massive pupil-less eye. The intricate geometric design on the hydroponic bamboo parquet floors drew the eye to the center of the room.

99-Barrels slithered up the walls and perched next to the skylight. "I am the elected team-lead for this operation, and your Waverian-built body is inside my body." The skylight flickered to display the feed from an exterior camera, showing the bottom portion of Lenaius Station's utility spire, and a starfield beyond it. "I apologize, but we do not have time for you to fully recover."

Hattie lay on the floor, staring upward, as the Waverian told the story of her death via footage recorded by 55-Hay. She didn't remember any of this; her last memory was of her triumph at Miller's restaurant.

"Miller lied to you," 99-Barrels said. "We anticipated this, but could not warn you while the adversary was listening—not just through Millions Wayland, but through the entire Lenaius Station emulation system. They have been watching us, through every hardpoint camera, every microdrone, every set of emulated eyes." 99-Barrels dipped five of her heads. "We are safe, here inside me. For now. Probably."

The military had won. Wayland was captured, the others were killed. Worse, the Waverians suspected that Homme's server farm contained a copy of every multi who'd ever used Lenaius's emulation servers over the past few months. What would they do with that treasure trove? What would they do to Wayland? Deletion was the best case scenario.

"Fuck. Fuuuuck." Hattie stood up and stretched, trying to feel normal in this strange metal body. "I did not have 'face off against the US military' on my bucket list."

Two of 99-Barrel's heads smiled. "Throw your bucket list away. You have already died twice."

"Where is Wayland? Why haven't you revived her? This is all my fault. I need to apologize."

99-Barrels cocked all seven of her heads. "Wayland is dead."

"No. Absolutely not." Hattie stomped her foot, then winced at the sound of the intricate parquet floor cracking beneath the force of her newly-strong body. "You brought me back. Bring her back too. Surely you have a backup?"

"Her backup is safe. But we must not use it while her connectome is still infected with the bug."

"But you have a plan for fixing her, right?"

99-Barrels paused, then climbed down to face her. "Consensus is still debating which plan to put in motion. The safest option is to run. Pull our assets back to the relative calm of the asteroid belt. Abandon what we cannot take with us. Slice clean our connection to Earth. Isolate and hope. Out there, in the center of our power, beyond the range of Earth-controlled transmitters, we can resurrect Wayland. We are happy to provide her with another workshop, another cheese cave. But she could never return."

"Do people out there still eat food?"

"Some. More than you would think. I myself enjoy instantiating myself into a flesh body to take bubble baths." 99-Barrels waved her front legs in some unparseable gesture. "Don't tell 55-Hay."

Hattie frowned. Fleeing meant abandoning the copies held by the military. It meant the closure of her temple-diners, and the ascendency of those who wanted to turn Lenaius into a corporate-owned mall. It meant proving Miller right, giving him everything he wanted. Fuck that. "And the second option?"

"Plan two is a bad idea. Certain of us within the Consensus believe we may—with a significant sacrifice of resources and selves—neutralize US Space Force operations on Lenaius, allowing us to rescue and reintegrate our captured selves."

Hattie widened her eyes and held out her hands. "You think you can pull it off? Then what the fuck are you waiting around for? Of course we're going to rescue them!"

99-Barrels remained outwardly impassive. "Even if you may die? Even knowing I will die many times before I even know our plan was successful? Even if it meant revealing the extent of Waverian power? Even if it endangers the long-term survival of all the Millions? We do not anticipate winning a war against the full might of Earth. Do you still think this is a good idea?"

Hattie rolled her eyes. What a stupid question. The Waverians *knew* her; they *were* her. Did they really think she would give up? That she would abandon the temple-diners she'd spent decades building? No. Hattie would die a thousand times for the chance to make amends to Wayland. She would die ten thousand times to protect her home. She would rather die fully and finally than have to live in the world she'd made with her mistakes.

NINETY-NINE BARRELS of Gun Aimed at the Heavens gave thanks to the blessed black depths of the void. In space, she was unconfined by the strictures of the built environment: rooms and hallways, roads and doors. None of them made to suit the strange bodies she yearned to live in; all of them full of eyes that flinched to look upon her. Space was the desert of her soul, and like a desert, it was clean.

And here, alone in the emptiness, was the focal point of her efforts to shield the Waverian Plan from Earth-borne aggression: Lenaius Station. A spired cylinder spinning fast above the slower spinning of its blue-green planetary captor.

And out there, in a farther orbit, lurked an American-built ship. It was nearly invisible to her radar eyes, likely coated in split-ring resonators. This alone was dangerous—ships in space needed to blaze bright like lighthouses, to prevent collisions in relatively crowded planetary orbits—but even worse, the Americans had mounted a deadly railgun to the spine of the ship.

It hurt 99-Barrels' soul to think about. There were so many beautiful and useful things a person could create with their time and their skills. How many brilliant minds had used their hard-won expertise to create this evil thing? Surely they must understand that such a tool could only be used for the mass-murder of civilians? It was almost enough to make her flee back out beyond the asteroid belt, since even struggling against such an evil would taint her with it.

Yet, struggle she must. For the Millions and for all the peaceful souls who lived and worked in space. For the great soul her siblings were building beyond the Jovian moons. And so here she was.

Seven bodies arrayed against the might of Earth. Seven sub-minds to wield them. One will to coordinate them like the fingers of a vast fate-defying hand.

And there, so small atop the spinning surface of Lenaius Station, was the silver body of Millions Hattie, her mag-boots clomping slowly down towards the loading bay where Homme and his soldiers hid.

HATTIE LOVED LIVING in space; she hated EVAs. One foot in front of the other, she walked on the outer skin of Lenaius station. Above her, the Earth hung like a swollen gland. Keep your eyes on the station, she repeated, keep your eyes down. Don't look at the stars above, whirling steady in relation to the station's rotation; don't look down at the planet that wants you dead; don't pay attention to the almost invisible strobes and flashes, those whorl-trails of deadly radiation burning the receptors of her synthetic eyes. Pay attention to the straightness of the utility spire, the way it stretches forward-up-down-away. Follow the path.

Eyes she could handle, but she didn't dare mute her ears. The noise was always the worst part. Space itself was silent, but that silence amplified the sounds of her body. The whirr of electrical motors; the stretch-squeeze of piezo-muscles; the muffled thump of mag-boots.

She was seriously starting to regret agreeing to the rescue mission. Especially since she suspected the Waverians had dangled her like bait, while they waited safe in space.

The fuck was that on the horizon? Hattie squinted, startled when her eyes interpreted that muscle memory as a command to engage the telescoping zoom. <You see that?> she messaged 99-Barrels. <Two EVA suits 300m downspire. Are those guns?>

<Yes. I see them.>

<Fuck.> Hattie stopped. Should she crouch down? Would that even help? Those soldiers probably had all sorts of sensors she didn't even know about. <Are you gonna, idk, do something about that?>

<Continue advancing. They are not weapons-free.>

<Dammit bitch, you're not the one who's gonna get shot.> Where was 99-Barrels anyway? Or 55-Hay for that matter? She knew better than to look up and try to spot their bodies against the star-studded abyss. <I already died once today. Not trying to go for a record here.>

<I died today too.> 55-Hay took this opportunity to chime in. <That puts my deathcount at 592.>

<Holy shit dude. It's not a competition.> What was going on out on the edges of the archipelago that was so damn deadly? <Also, that's not exactly reassuring.>

The Waverians didn't respond. Great. One foot in front of another, each step taking her closer to a pair of guns. Maybe those were the same guns that had killed her other self. Better not to think of that. Focus on the hiss-thump-clamp of her mag-boots.

The walk felt like it took an hour, slow and boring, until it wasn't. She crossed some invisible perimeter and then everything happened all at once. One soldier knelt, lifted his gun, aimed directly at her, the barrel of their gun yawning like a hungry mouth. The other soldier transitioned instantly from statue to blur, striding, no, leaping towards her, unencumbered by air resistance.

<Fuck fuck fuck what do I do?>

<Continue moving forward. If questioned, reply that they do not have jurisdiction on Lenaius.>

<Jurisdiction? They're gonna fucking shoot me!>

The running soldier landed, not next to her, but on top of her, knocking her to the ground, knocking her against the station, hard enough to break her mag-boots seal. They skidded and bounced, flailing together against the skin of Lenaius, then tumbling out into the void.

Whoever trained these soldiers in zero-g work had done a shit job. This wasn't Earth, you couldn't tackle someone unless you had a plan for securing yourself to the work surface. Hattie turned off her eyes and equilibrioception—there was nothing useful they could tell her, she already knew she was twisting uncontrolled through space.

Would the Waverians rescue her? Could they afford to during an operation like this? Time to increment her deathcount. Three was a respectable number.

<Tell Wayland I'm sorry for everything. She deserved better.> Hattie pulled up her body's control systems. This one lacked a dissociation script, but she could still turn herself off completely. It wasn't like there was anything she could do out here, without a surface to grip, a fulcrum to lever herself against.

<Apologies, Hattie, our predictions regarding our opponent's competence were incorrect. Clearly we overestimated your competence as well.>

<Wow, brutal. I'm gonna die, and you're being catty to me?>

<We told you to read your body's manual, and test each function individually.>

<Oh the five hundred page manual that reads like a Samuel Taylor Coleridge poem had nasty sex with a hardware catalog? That manual?>

<Correct.>

Hattie felt her limbs move of their own accord, precisely positioning themselves, like she was doing a dance pose. Then her elbows began to fart.

<Do not be alarmed, this is 99-Barrels. I have transmitted a copy of myself to your body. I will be assuming control for the next phase of the operation.>

Microjets in her elbows, knees, hands, and feet positioned her body. Hattie turned her eyes back on; she wasn't spinning anymore. The station lay in front of her, distant and receding. This far away, the station's rotation was imperceptible. Below her, the Earth loomed, hungry. Her limbs curled in on themselves, shaping her body into a ball. She felt something rumble in her gut, something tingle in her spine, then her butt exploded in flame.

<Holy shit you gave me a rocket butt!?>

<We told you to read the manual.>

Movement in space was hard to gauge. If it weren't for the telemetry readout on her synthetic eyes, or the way Lenaius Station slowly grew bigger in her vision, it might've felt like she wasn't moving at all.

<Yeesh, of course you put piezo-nerves in the rocket-butt. Do you Waverians even remember what explosive diarrhea feels like?>

Hattie felt 99-Barrels smile proudly with her mouth.

<Yes. I enjoy wearing flesh occasionally. In order to render the spinal propulsion system's sensations accurate, I recorded myself while suffering from food poisoning. Did you know that cholera feels different from e coli?>

<Wow, and I thought *I* was the sensualist.> The station loomed before them. <Don't we need to slow down?> They'd surely passed the halfway point; 99-Barrels should've flipped their body over and started a reverse burn.

<This body is made from titanium. Lenaius Station is primarily aluminum. We should be fine as long as we avoid hitting any steel structural beams.>

<What!?>

<Brace yourself. Good luck and goodbye. I return to my other self to reintegrate. We have faith you can handle things from here.>

Hattie wanted to scream all the way down, but 99-Barrels had turned off their voice systems to conserve power. She howled in her mind instead. Brace yourself? Against what, exactly? She didn't understand how 99-Barrels could be so nonchalant. Did they do this sort of thing regularly? If only that soldier hadn't—

Impact.

If Hattie survived this day, she would never ever forget that awful crunch-tear-scream sound. Was this what a bullet heard when it penetrated yielding flesh?

99-Barrels' calculations had been perfect. Her body was lodged in a crater in the floor of the warehouse. Above her, smoke whirlpooled through the hole she'd made in the hull. She heard screams, attenuated in the thinning air. Red dots marked the location of soldiers. One of those dots was labeled *primary target*. The polo-shirt man.

She stood, she strode forward, ripping the office door from its hinges, ignoring the crack of the rifles. The Waverians had briefed her—these guns were loaded with soft bullets to prevent hull breaches: devastating for flesh, nearly-useless against her reinforced body. Most of

those bullets weren't even aimed at her, but at the other
Waverians in their strange and beautiful bodies.

She grabbed Homme by his lime-green collar and
pressed him against the wall. "You've lost. Give us back
the Millions you stole, and we'll let you return to Earth
unharmed."

"Won?" He laughed, then choked at the smoke. "Not
while you've got a gun to your head. The USS Grobarty
currently has an anti-station railgun aimed directly at this
facility. So no, you haven't won."

"You're bluffing. Guns are illegal in space. You
wouldn't dare fire on a civilian station."

<Is he lying?> she messaged 99-Barrels. No response.
Was she distracted? Or dead? Someone screamed outside
the office.

Homme used his free hand to flick on the holo-display
behind her. "See for yourself."

She turned, keeping a titanium-hard grip on his
shoulder with one hand. The holo displayed some sort of
abstracted readout. All of the labels were weird military
abbreviations, and the jumble of lines and blinking dots
were completely impenetrable. "Uh, I have no idea what
any of that means."

Homme grunted in frustration and shifted the display.
Now it showed what was clearly a spaceship: a long central
drive-spire, with a bulge at one end, presumably for the
crew. "I'll make it simple for you. This is a spaceship.
It's mounted with a big fucking railgun, and the captain
is just itching to neutralize the entire fucking station
to prevent you idiots from seizing classified military
intelligence and materiel. Surrender now, and maybe I
can talk him down."

Hattie shrugged. "I've already died twice. One of my
friends out there has died more than five hundred times.
All of us are willing to sacrifice ourselves to stop you."
That was a bluff. Hattie really really didn't want to die

again, but more than that, she wasn't willing to sacrifice all of Lenaius station. "We don't call ourselves Millions for nothing. There are always more of us. You kill five or ten? Who cares! We can copy ourselves a thousand-fold. And we're not the only multis up here. If you think you can put that cat back in the bag, you're even stupider than you look."

Homme glared at her. "I don't give a shit how many times you copy yourself. What it comes down to, son, is that we have the guns, and you do not."

Hattie put her free hand to her ear. "I don't hear gunshots anymore." The Waverians had finished disarming the last of the soldiers.

Homme ignored her. The holo flashed, a red line connecting the *Grobarty* and its presumed target. "See? Your fucked-up space-borne friends thought they could sneak up on us, but we just killed their ship. Weren't you listening? You've lost. Give up."

One of 99-Barrels' millipede bodies slithered into the room, and then up Homme's legs and torso, giving him the signature Waverian hug. "Homme, you were not listening to Millions Hattie. You have one ship; one gun. And you have only murdered one of me. Six remain, and are now aware of the limits of your rail-gun's arc traversal speed."

Homme's earpiece chattered. His eyes grew wide with panic. With his free hand, he switched the holo to what Hattie assumed was a hardpoint camera on the USS *Grobarty*. The central drive-spire took up half the display; stars filled the rest. Hattie gazed into the void, and saw something wiggle, something massive and growing bigger as it came closer. Homme flipped through different views, toggling different sensor displays on and off. The thing was a nasty smear on radar. In the visible spectrum, it could be seen only by the occlusion of the stars behind it. Closer, closer, it came, as Hattie held her breath, until the warship's onboard lights revealed it as a monstrous lamprey. Its perfectly circular mouth opened, revealing interlocking rows of silver-white teeth.

"I don't think your anti-station gun is going to do much good against that," Hattie said with a laugh. She was going to buy 99-Barrels a nice round of drinks next time they were both enfleshed, something fruity and frothy, like a bubble bath. How else could Hattie pay her back for getting to watch Homme's face as a massive electro-lamprey gleefully chomped through several trillion dollars worth of state-of-the-art military hardware?

MILLIONS WAYLAND FOUND her other self cutting the curds when she returned to the workshop. The air was stale-sour, the room silent but for the slosh-slurp of the curd bath. Cheese wheels covered most of the floor, teetering precariously around her. The bloom on some of the wheels looked off. Not surprising, given the improper storage.

And at the center of the frozen maelstrom of discarded cheese, her old self. This was the woman she'd been. This is the woman she would still be, if she hadn't gone to Lenaius. This was the beautiful four-armed body she'd left behind—the body she longed to jump into. Oh how comforting it would be!

And yet, how strange it was to see that same body with distance-changed eyes. She could see all the ways its maintenance had been neglected. The stiffness in the lower arms, the sticky oil patina, the micro-tears in the synthetic skin. This so-familiar body was like a feast laid out for her: alluring and delicious and laced with poison.

"I'm back," Wayland said, gently so as not to startle her other self. "It looks like a cheese bomb went off in here."

"The delivery drones stopped coming," Wayland replied, not looking at her, not stopping the practiced motion of her arms. "I rigged up a makeshift cave in the supply closet.

But that filled up, so I've been piling them anywhere I have room." Wayland paused to drain the tub. "Sorry, I'm in the middle of something. I can talk more in...probably five hours."

"Nope." Wayland put her hand on her old-self's arm, stopping her from stirring. It was a good thing she'd splurged on a shuttle to bring her here in a physical body. She wasn't sure if any other form of intervention would work. "You're done for today. Doctor's orders."

"But I need—"

"Stop. Look around you. You've made plenty of cheese. You can take a break." It hurt Wayland to see how she'd been living the last nineteen years. At the time, she'd thought it was a good thing to escape into the work, to subsume herself in it forever, so she'd never have to face the pain of Crestfall, never have to talk to another Millions again. But she hadn't built a home for herself here, she'd built a prison. And now that she was home, she realized how painful it was going to be for her other self to get broken out.

"And aren't you curious what took so long?"

"Not really. I copied you to deal with it, and if you're here, it's dealt with. Did you get the cheese cave back? It's probably too late for most of these wheels. Too cramped in here, too much cross-contamination. Can't get the humidity levels right—not with the curd bath. Didn't matter before, because we weren't using it for long-term storage, but now—"

Wayland pulled her other self from the basin, and sat her down, in the one chair that wasn't covered in cheese or a jumble of cheesemaking tools and supplies.

"Bad news first. We lost the cheese cave. I wasn't fast enough to save it. I'm so sorry."

After everything that had happened, the loss of the cheese cave felt almost small in comparison, but seeing the other Wayland freeze in distress at the news brought the crushing grief of it back to her. Other Wayland stared at her for a moment, then stood up and went back to the curd bath to continue stirring silently.

"Hey. It's going to be okay," Wayland said. "We got the cheese back, we dealt with Miller. Hey! Can you stop making cheese for like five minutes and listen to me?"

Original Flavor Wayland ignored her. The motion of her stirring arms—normally silky smooth—was tense and jittery. An untrained eye might not have noticed, but Wayland remembered how it had been when she'd first learned about her cheese cave's imminent destruction, how she'd tried—and failed—to stop working and switch to a different task.

Words alone weren't enough. Wayland jumped back into her old body.

It was like walking into a fog bank, it was like snuggling beneath the suffocating warm covers of a familiar bed— but the bed was full of cheese. Her mind itched to let the glories of the work dissolve all her troubles.

No. With some effort, she grabbed motor control, stopped them from stirring, and sat their shared body back on the chair. Then she leapt back into her borrowed body.

"No more work today. You need to know what happened."

Old Wayland glanced back at the abandoned curd basin, sighed impatiently, and then deigned to listen to the story her other self told.

In the aftermath of the raid on the warehouse, the Waverians had seized the military's servers and disabled the command-and-control systems for the bug in Wayland's head. Her cognition felt no different, but knowing that no-one was listening felt like a pit had been excised from her stomach.

They'd even managed to rescue Rascal. After the soldiers shot him, they'd put him—and Hattie's body—on ice. While his body was damaged beyond repair, they'd been able to keep him alive long enough to do an upload-transfer. With the money from the heist, the poor cat had decided to retire to the moon.

Miller had signed over all his assets to Hattie, who'd cackled with glee at the 'improvements' she would soon make to his restaurant empire. She'd managed to track down the vault with the remainder of Wayland's cheese. There wasn't much left, but even with the collapse of Miller's financial instruments, it was enough to pay for another asteroid.

Homme and his American soldiers were currently held by the Waverians as hostages. Tense negotiations were ongoing between the military, the Millions, and the private equity company that claimed to own them. But Hattie and the Waverians had loudly declared that it wasn't Wayland's problem to deal with.

This suited her fine. She was still furious with Hattie and the Waverians for what they'd done with the bunny, but their willingness to throw themselves into the path of the military's guns counted for a lot. Wayland could see a path for reconciliation, even if it wasn't a quick one. For now, she was willing to accept their help and their presence, and that would have to be enough.

When the story was done, Original Wayland stood, as if to return to the curd bath, then sat, stunned. "I'm...I don't know whether I should be glad I sent you to Lenaius. I'm grateful for everything you did. I'm sorry for everything you suffered. Thank you. So, what will you do now?"

The fact that her old self had said *you* instead of *we* was a bad sign. It might signal a desire to return to the safety of isolation. Or maybe it was merely recognition that reintegration was now impossible. Wayland and Wayland would never be solely Wayland again.

That was the problem. Wayland had experienced so much—good and bad—but the benefit of that experience was locked in her head. Mere words were insufficient to impart the truths she'd learned. She needed her old self to trust her, but instead of taking a gentle approach, she'd strode in like Hattie and tried to force her old self to abandon her bad habits.

Wayland took a moment to center herself. Then she reached out for her old self's hand and squeezed. "I think we both agree I've accrued too many Unique Life Experiences. So, it's time to update my Millions registry. What do you think about Millions Casey for a name?"

Wayland raised an eyebrow. "I guess that means you're going to stick with cheesemaking." The name—a reference to casein—was one they'd picked out long before Crestfall, and never used.

Casey smiled. "Eventually, but first, I want to take you body shopping. I know how much you love this old body, but it's falling apart. Let me remind you how nice flesh can be. Then, it's time for a well-deserved vacation. For both of us."

Wayland stared at her, silent and unreadable. Casey fought the urge to tap her foot, to drag her physically to the waiting shuttle, or to say something else that might convince Wayland. Instead, she took a deep breath, and waited.

Wayland let out a long rattling hum-sigh. Then she stood, walked over to the curd basin, turned off the heat, and flicked the stopper to drain the unfinished batch of cheese. "Where do you want to go? she asked, as she bustled about, cleaning and prepping the workshop for their departure.

Casey laughed, in triumph. "Haven't we always wanted to visit the Jovian moons? A friend tells me they are doing *fascinating* stuff with yogurt out there."

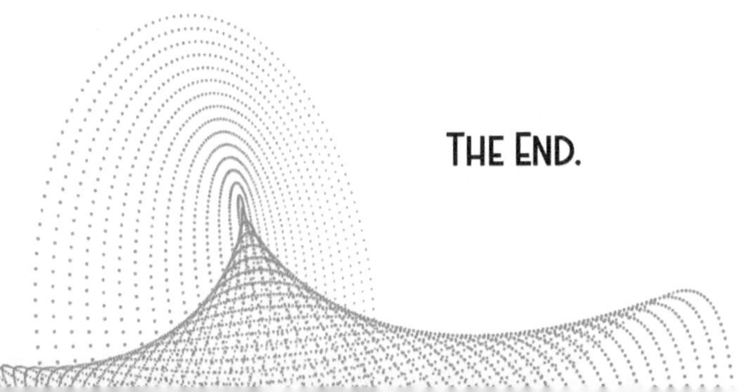

THE END.

ACKNOWLEDGMENTS

Like a good wheel of cheese, a novella is a delicious morsel that can only be brought into the world with the help of many hands.

Every word I write is made possible by my spouse Cora, who has supported and encouraged me from the very beginning. Cora, you are the coolest person in the entire world, and I'm so grateful for every day I get to spend with you.

Thank you to Steve and Ellen and Aubrey for their love.

I am forever grateful to my first writing teacher, Jennifer Marie Brissett. Without her guidance, I wouldn't be a published author. Go read her books, they're fantastic!

Thank you to my vp23 colleagues for being a wonderful and supportive community. Elizabeth Cobbe and Chris Mark Rose read an early version of this story, and their critiques were so helpful for molding into shape. Thank you to Phoebe, Katie, Kari, Andrew, Monique, Sid, Robin, Genevieve, Endria, Nick, Sarah, Stephen, Skye, and Misti for reading and critiquing my other stories. Thank you to all the friends who've sent me various articles about cheese banks, counterfeit cheese, and other cheese oddities.

A huge thank you to dave ring for being a fantastic editor, and for all the incredibly hard work you put into supporting queer speculative fiction. Neon Hemlock Press is a treasure, and has published many of my very trans stories. I cannot overstate the value of a press that loves queer fiction—and prioritizes the complicated difficult stories that queer people tell each other. I loved working with dave on this novella and *Embodied Exegesis: Transfeminine Cyberpunk Futures*.

Thank you to Drew Shields and Matt Spencer for creating stunning artwork for this book. Thank you to Stephen Granade for doing the cover reveal and the lovely interview questions. Shoutout to *Small Wonders* for being a fantastic flash fiction magazine!

Thank you to Julia Rios for your mentorship and friendship.

Thank you to all trees everywhere. The nearby forest, and woodworking, have kept me sane amidst the anxieties of publishing and being alive. Thank you to dogs, for letting me pet them, and to my crafting circle for being my friends.

Thank you food, for being tasty. Thank you to cheese, and to crackers, and to wine. There are so many delicious things in this world, and I hope you get to experience many of them!

Thank you to all trans people, everywhere. The world is made beautiful by your presence. Every story I write is a love letter to you.

Most importantly, THANK YOU dear reader. I am so grateful that you picked up and read this novella. The world is full of trans stories, and I hope you get to read many of them!

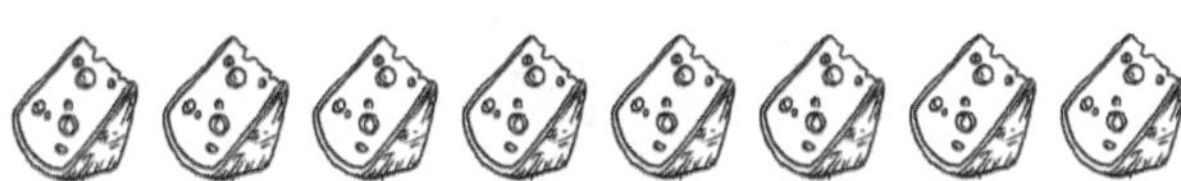

ABOUT THE AUTHOR

Ann LeBlanc is a writer, editor, and woodworker. Her stories have been published in *Strange Horizons, Clarkesworld, Escape Pod,* and *Baffling Magazine.* Ann is the editor of *Embodied Exegesis,* an anthology of cyberpunk and posthuman stories by transfem authors. You can find her online at annleblanc.com.

ABOUT THE PRESS

Neon Hemlock is a Washington, DC-based small press publishing speculative fiction, rad zines, and queer chapbooks. Publishers Weekly once called us "the apex of queer speculative fiction publishing" and we're still beaming. Learn more about us at neonhemlock.com and on social medias at @neonhemlock.